THIS DIARY BELONGS TO:

# Nikki J. Maxwell

*PRIVATE & CONFIDENTIAL*

If found, please return to ME for REWARD!

(NO SNOOPING ALLOWED!!! ☹)

## Also by
## Rachel Renée Russell

### DORK DIARIES

| | |
|---|---|
| Dork Diaries | TV Star |
| Party Time | Once Upon a Dork |
| Pop Star | Drama Queen |
| Skating Sensation | Puppy Love |
| Dear Dork | Frenemies Forever |
| Holiday Heartbreak | Crush Catastrophe |

How to Dork Your Diary

OMG!: All About Me Diary!

Dork Diaries

Dork Diaries #2

Dork Diaries #3

Dork Diaries #4

### THE MISADVENTURES OF MAX CRUMBLY

Locker Hero

Middle School Mayhem

# Rachel Renée Russell

## Double DORK diaries 5

SIMON AND SCHUSTER

First published as an omnibus edition in Great Britain in 2019 by Simon & Schuster UK Ltd
A CBS COMPANY
Simon & Schuster UK Ltd
1st Floor, 222 Gray's Inn Road, London WC1X 8HB

Dork Diaries: Drama Queen first published in Great Britain in 2015 by Simon & Schuster UK Ltd, a CBS company. Originally published in 2015 in the USA as Dork Diaries: Tales from a Not-So-Dorky Drama Queen, by Aladdin, an imprint of Simon & Schuster Children's Publishing Division.

Dork Diaries: Puppy Love first published in Great Britain in 2015 by Simon & Schuster UK Ltd, a CBS company. Originally published in 2015 in the USA as Dork Diaries: Tales from a Not-So-Perfect Sitter, by Aladdin, an imprint of Simon & Schuster Children's Publishing Division.

A CIP catalogue record for this book
is available from the British Library.

ISBN 978-1-4711-8234-1

www.simonandschuster.co.uk
www.simonandschuster.com.au
www.dorkdiaries.co.uk

3 5 7 9 10 8 6 4

Printed and bound by CPI Group (UK) Ltd, Croydon, CR0 4YY

MIX
Paper from
responsible sources
FSC® C020471

Simon & Schuster UK Ltd are committed to sourcing paper
that is made from wood grown in sustainable forests and support the Forest
Stewardship Council, the leading international forest certification organisation.
Our books displaying the FSC logo are printed on FSC certified paper.

# TOTAL DISASTER!!!

Mean girl Mackenzie has stolen Nikki's diary!
Now in a dorky twist, Mackenzie spills all
the details of her own GLAMFABULOUS life!

Find out what the queen bee

really thinks about Nikki and her

friends in DRAMA QUEEN . . .

The past twenty-four hours of my life have been so disgustingly NAUSEATING that I'm actually starting to feel like a . . . puddle of . . . um, cat . . . VOMIT!!

First I ruined my brand-new sweater with a PBJ and pickle sandwich (a long story).

Then I got hit in the face by a dodgeball during gym in front of the ENTIRE class and ended up trapped in a wacky fairy tale (an even longer story!).

Okay, I can handle the utter HUMILIATION of walking around school OBLIVIOUS to the fact that a SANDWICH is stuck to my abdomen like duct tape.

Hey, I can even handle a mild concussion. However, what I CAN'T handle is the fact that "someone" started an AWFUL rumor about me!

I overheard two CCP (Cute, Cool & Popular) girls gossiping about it in the bathroom.

Rumor has it that my CRUSH kissed me (at a charity event last weekend) on a DARE merely to snag a FREE large pizza from Queasy Cheesy!

Of course I totally FREAKED when I heard it! Not only is a dare like that rude and insensitive, but it's a very cruel joke to play on a person like . . . well . . . ME!

I was SURE the whole thing was a big fat LIE! Sorry! But everyone knows Queasy Cheesy pizzas are just NASTY! Had it been a dare for a yummy Crazy Burger, I'd TOTALLY believe it!

Hey, I'll be the first to admit, that rumor could have been A LOT worse. But STILL . . . !! I just wish "someone" would stay out of my personal business. And by "someone," I mean my mortal enemy . . . MACKENZIE HOLLISTER ☹!!

I don't know why that girl HATES MY GUTS! It wasn't MY fault Principal Winston gave her a three-day detention for "unsportsmanlike behavior" for slamming me in the face with that dodgeball.

I'm really LUCKY I'm not in a COMA right now!
Or undergoing life-threatening surgery . . .

Anyway, as punishment for what MacKenzie did to me, she has to clean the bug-infested showers in the girls' locker room.

Unfortunately, I learned today that the bug problem in there is REALLY bad!!

I was sitting behind MacKenzie in French class finishing up my homework when I noticed there was something stuck in her hair.

At first I thought it was one of those fancy designer barrettes she loves to wear. But when I took a closer look, I realized it was actually a gigantic dead STINK BUG!! EWW ☹!!

That's when I tapped her on the shoulder. "Um, MacKenzie! Excuse me, but I just wanted to let you know that—"

"Nikki, WHY are you even talking to me?! Just mind your OWN business!" she said, glaring at me like I was something her spoiled poodle, Fifi, had left in the grass in her backyard.

4

MACKENZIE, GLARING AT ME
IN A VERY RUDE MANNER!

"Okay! Then I won't tell you there's a huge dead STINK BUG in your hair!" I said very calmly. "Besides, it kinda looks like an ugly barrette! And it totally complements your eye color!"

"WHAT?!" MacKenzie gasped, and her eyes got as big as saucers.

She whipped out her makeup mirror.

"OMG! OMG! There's a big black . . . INSECT with prickly legs tangled in my golden tresses! EEEEEEEEEEEK!!!" she shrieked. Then she started jumping around hysterically and shaking her hair to get it out. She had a complete meltdown!

"You're making it worse. Now it's even more tangled in there. Just sit down and chillax!" I said as I grabbed a tissue and reached for her hair.

"GET AWAY FROM ME!!" she screamed. "I don't want TWO disgusting CREATURES in my beautiful hair!"

"Stop acting like a spoiled BRAT!" I shot back.
"I'm just removing the bug for you! See?!"

ME, REMOVING THE STINK BUG
FROM MACKENZIE'S HAIR

"That is DISGUSTING! Get it away from me!"

"You're welcome!" I said, glaring at her.

"Hmph! Don't expect a thank-you from me! It's all YOUR fault that bug was in my hair! It's probably from those nasty showers I'm being forced to clean."

Suddenly she folded her arms and narrowed her eyes at me.

"Or maybe YOU put it in my hair to try to ruin my reputation! I bet you want everyone to think my house is overrun with disgusting bugs! Again."

"MacKenzie, I think your lip gloss must be leaking into your brain. That's ridiculous!"

"How could you put that nasty BUG in my hair?! I'm getting SICK just thinking about it. UGH!!"

Then she covered her mouth and mumbled something. But I couldn't understand a word. . . .

8

ME, TRYING TO FIGURE OUT WHAT
MACKENZIE WAS SAYING!

Although we were in French class, it definitely
didn't sound like she was speaking French!

By the time I FINALLY figured out what she was saying, it was TOO late.

Desperate, she took off running toward the wastebasket at the front of the room.

But, unfortunately, she DIDN'T make it.

I could NOT believe that MacKenzie Hollister, the QUEEN of the CCPs, actually threw up in front of the ENTIRE French class!

She was like a bad car accident! I really DIDN'T want to see her covered in puke from head to toe ☹! But I couldn't help staring ☺!

I have never seen her SO embarrassed. SO humiliated. SO vulnerable. SO um . . . MESSY!

I was both shocked and surprised when I was suddenly overcome with overwhelming emotion.

I had NEVER, EVER felt more SORRY for a human being in my ENTIRE life! . . .

POOR CHUCK THE JANITOR!!
HE HAS A REALLY DIRTY JOB!

It seemed like such a grave injustice that HE had to clean up the horrible mess that MacKenzie had made.

Sometimes life is SO UNFAIR ☹!!

But he took his job very seriously because he actually put on one of those paper mask thingies that doctors wear during surgery.

I'm guessing it was probably because of the very noxious and excessive . . . STINKAGE!

Anyway, our French teacher immediately sent MacKenzie down to the office to call her parents to go home for the rest of the day.

And instead of having class in our smelly, contaminated room, our teacher took us down to the library to quietly study our French vocabulary words.

Which was PERFECT for me because I was able to work on my special project for National Library Week later this month.

My BFFs, Chloe and Zoey, and I held a book drive for our school back in September, and it was a HUGE success.

So now we're planning an even bigger one for National Library Week!

We'll also be traveling to NYC for a book festival and will get to "Meet-n-Greet" some of our favorite authors. SQUEEEEEEE!!!

Anyway, I can't believe MacKenzie ACTUALLY thinks I put that stink bug in her hair!!

Unfortunately for her, it looks like the kids in our class are already GOSSIPING about what happened.

One girl had her cell phone out. She showed it to a guy, and then they started snickering like crazy.

I guessed that she was probably texting the ENTIRE school!

But this whole thing is all MacKenzie's fault!!

13

She totally OVERREACTED and FREAKED OUT
even after I offered to help her.

MacKenzie is such a VOMIT QUEEN!

OOPS! I meant . . .

# DRAMA QUEEN!

Sorry about that, MacKenzie!!

☺!!

I'm SO upset right now I can barely write ☹!!
I was at my locker, minding my own business, when
MacKenzie tapped me on my shoulder and sneered,
"Why are YOU always hanging around here?!!
PLEASE! Just go away!"

"Sorry, but I hang around here because, unfortunately,
MY locker is right next to YOURS," I said, rolling my
eyes at her.

"I still can't believe you put that bug in my hair!
I'll NEVER speak to you again as long as I live!!"

"Whatever, MacKenzie!" I muttered as I counted
down in my head for her to start blabbing at me
again. Five . . . four . . . three . . . two . . .

"You're MAD at me because I spilled the beans that
Brandon kissed you on a DARE just to get a free
pizza! And now everyone is gossiping about it. So
to get even, you PRETENDED to be injured in gym
class just to get ME in trouble! . . ."

"NIKKI, YOU'RE JUST A PATHETIC FAKE!"

Sorry, but I could only take so much of Miss Thang talking TRASH right to my face like that! So I got all up in HER face and said . . .

"Really, MacKenzie?! You think I'M faking?!!
Does this BRUISE look FAKE to you?! I don't
think so! The ONLY fake things around here,
girlfriend, are YOUR bad hair extensions and
tacky spray-on tan!!"

ME, SHOWING MACKENZIE MY BRUISE

"Poor baby! So, I'm supposed to feel guilty when I actually did you a big FAVOR?" MacKenzie snarled. "That cute little bruise I gave you draws attention away from your hideous face!"

"Um, MacKenzie, have you looked at YOUR face lately? What brand of makeup did you use this morning? Paint-by-number?!"

"I wouldn't go there if I were you. My designer lipstick cost MORE than your entire ugly outfit. So don't HATE me because I'm BEAUTIFUL!"

"Well, you need to EAT some of your designer lipstick. Then MAYBE you'll be BEAUTIFUL on the INSIDE!" I shot back.

Suddenly MacKenzie got SUPERserious and stared at my forehead.

"Nikki, I'm really worried about that bruise. It looks like gangrene might be setting in. I need to run down to the nurse's office and get some bandages for you. Wait right here, okay, hon?"

But I already knew what was going on in that TWISTED little BRAIN of hers. . . .

← ME

MACKENZIE, PUTTING A
BANDAGE ON MY BRUISE!

When she got done with me, I was going to look like a . . . totally messed up . . . middle school, um . . . . MUMMY!

And I was NOT about to let MacKenzie publicly HUMILIATE me! Again!

It was bad enough that she was spreading a nasty rumor about me. But now I was worried she was going to ruin my friendship with Brandon.

Anyway, I was getting my books out of my locker and still FUMING about everything she'd done to me, when I felt ANOTHER tap on my shoulder!

JUST GREAT ☹!! The last thing I wanted to deal with right then was a second round of harassment from MacKenzie. I was so NOT letting her put bandages on my bruise!

That's when I totally lost it! I wanted to shove her bandages right down her throat. But since I don't believe in violence, I decided to just tell her off in a very RUDE yet friendly way. . . .

20

OMG!! When I turned around and saw it was BRANDON, I totally FREAKED OUT!!

His mouth dropped open and he looked hurt and confused. I guess I was in shock or something, because when I tried to explain why I'd said those things and apologize, all that came out was . . .

We just stood there. Very awkwardly. Staring at each other for what seemed like FOREVER!

"Okay, Nikki. If that's what you really want," he finally said quietly. "I guess I was totally out of line last weekend when I . . . . you know. Anyway, I owe you an apology. I'm very sorry."

"WHAT?! Brandon, I don't want or need your apology. What I'm trying to say is that I made a big mistake. Actually, I owe YOU an apolo—"

"Mistake?! Really?! Is that all it was to you?"

"Of course it was a mistake. I'd never do anything like that to you on purpose. It was a brief moment of stupidity and I'm sorry it happened. But it will NEVER happen again, I promise. You did NOT deserve that."

Brandon looked even more hurt than before.

It was almost like he didn't understand a word I was saying.

After another long silence, he took a deep breath and let out a sad sigh. "I really don't know what to say. . . ."

"Actually, Brandon, you don't have to say anything at all. I was really angry. And, as crazy as it sounds, I thought you were someone else."

"I know I could have been more honest with you. But I didn't mean to mislead you. Just don't be mad at me, okay?"

"You don't understand! I was actually mad at—"

"I DO understand, Nikki, and I want you to be happy. So I'll just back off, if that's what you really want."

He nervously brushed his shaggy bangs out of his eyes and glanced at his watch.

"Anyway, I think we BOTH better get to class. Later." Then he shoved his hands in his pockets and quickly walked away. . . .

ME, TOTALLY CONFUSED ABOUT WHAT JUST HAPPENED BETWEEN BRANDON AND ME ☹!

# MUST. NOT. PANIC!!!

Did I really just ACCIDENTALLY tell Brandon I was sick and tired of him making my life miserable and to go slither under a rock?!!

Yep! I think I actually DID!!

Okay, time to PANIC!!! . . .

# AAAAAAAAAAAAAHHH ☹!!!...
(That was me screaming!)

OMG! Like, WHO does that to their CRUSH?!!

I sighed, collapsed against my locker, and blinked back tears of frustration.

A massive wave of insecurity hung over me like a dark storm cloud as I carefully contemplated my next move:

1. Just "Shake It Off" and get to my geometry class since I had a quiz starting in less than two minutes (and I still needed to study) ☹!

26

2. Follow Brandon around the school "stalker-style" and apologize profusely until he finally accepts and agrees that we're best buds again.

3. Rush to the girls' bathroom, lock myself in a stall, and have a meltdown until Chloe and Zoey come and rescue me (AGAIN!).

4. Climb into my locker, slam the door shut, and stay in there SULKING until the last day of school or until I DIE of hunger, whichever occurs first!

I am the WORST! FRIEND!! EVER!!!

And now ~~I THINK~~ BRANDON HATES ME!!

☹!!

Today we only had a half day of school due to teacher training. Which means I didn't get a chance to talk to Chloe and Zoey about that big blowup I had with Brandon yesterday.

The crazy thing is that I think I'm more upset about it today than I was yesterday. Go figure!

I stopped by Brandon's locker a couple of times to try to talk to him, but he was never around.

So now I'm starting to suspect that he might be avoiding me. If I were him, I'd avoid me too!

I really want to believe MacKenzie made up that stupid rumor about the Prank-4-Pizza—but what if all (or some?) of it is actually TRUE ☹?!!

NONE of this makes sense! So in spite of all the craziness with Brandon yesterday, I'll still consider him a true friend. He deserves it.

The Brandon I know would NEVER, EVER accept a dare like that. And I REFUSE to waste any more of my time OBSESSING over it.

Anyway, after school I was doing my biology homework when my bratty little sister, Brianna, came skipping into my room, singing to herself.

"I've got a surprise! I've got a surprise!"

She poked her head over my shoulder to see what I was doing.

"Don't you wanna know what it is?" she asked.

"Nope," I answered indifferently, and continued reading.

"Well, I'm gonna show you anyway!"

That's when Brianna grinned and slammed a fishbowl on top of my biology book. Water splashed everywhere. My homework was completely soaked! . . .

BRIANNA, SPLASHING WATER ON
ME AND MY HOMEWORK!

Brianna!!" I yelled. "What are you doing?! Now my
book and homework are soaking wet! Go away!"

I took another look at the fishbowl and realized there was actually a goldfish in it.

"Where did THAT come from?"

"My teacher!" she replied. "She's letting ME babysit the class goldfish, Rover, for the entire weekend! We're gonna do lots of fun stuff together since we're best friends!"

All I could do was shake my head.

"Well, I think you need to be more careful with him. And more responsible. You could've cracked the fishbowl!"

"Responsible? What does that mean?" she asked.

"Let's see . . . how do I explain this in Nick Jr. terms?" I tapped my chin in thought. "I'll use Mom as an example. Mom feeds you, drives you to school, takes care of you when you're sick, and makes sure that you're always safe. That's called being responsible."

"Oh! NOW I understand. So, I need to be Rover's mommy!" she said eagerly.

"Yeah, something like that," I said. "Take him to your room and read him a story. I don't want any more water on my homework."

"Okeydokey!" she replied, and picked up her fishbowl. "Rover, your mommy is taking you to see her bedroom!"

I was glad she had that fish, because I figured it would keep her occupied and out of my hair.

But fifteen minutes later she came bouncing back into my room.

"Where's Rover?" I asked her.

"He's taking a bubble bath," she answered.

"WHAT?! Did you say BUBBLE BATH?!" I shrieked.

"Yep. He smelled really fishy, so I thought I'd give him a nice, warm bubble bath! That's what Mommy would do, right?"

"Brianna, are you serious?! Rover's a FISH! He's SUPPOSED to smell really fishy!"

"Well, he DOESN'T smell fishy anymore! Come take a sniff! I gotta go finish his bubble bath now. And dry him with your hair dryer. Bye!"

Oh . . . CRUD! I slammed my book shut and sighed. So much for homework!

I rushed down the hall and then peeked into the bathroom to check on poor Rover.

And, sure enough, it was just as I had feared.

He was covered in soap suds and bubbles and FLOATING in the bathroom sink!

Brianna was busy adding even more water. . . .

BRIANNA, GIVING HER
GOLDFISH A BUBBLE BATH!

"OMG! You really gave your goldfish a bubble bath? Are you crazy?!" I exclaimed. "Brianna, you cooked the darn thing!!"

"What are you talking about? Rover's really having fun. See how relaxed he is?"

EWW!!

Brianna stuck the dead fish right in my face. That's when I threw up in my mouth a little.

"He's FAR from relaxed!" I told Brianna. "He's not moving because he's . . . DEAD!"

"I'm his mommy, not you! And I say he's sleeping! So there!" she said, sticking her tongue out at me.

But when she asked me if Rover could borrow MY toothbrush so they could brush their teeth together at bedtime, I'd heard enough!

Obviously, something had to be done. If I let her learn the truth on her own, she'd probably need therapy for the rest of her life. Then again, Dad wasn't exactly the expert on topics like this. He'd probably just flush poor Rover down the toilet, which would be even more traumatizing to Brianna. I decided to talk to Mom about the dead fish situation tomorrow evening, as soon as she returned home from her visit with my grandma.

Sometimes having a NUTTY little sister is really challenging!! ☹!!

"Mom, do you know about Brianna's goldfish, Rover?" I asked.

"Yes, I do! And I think he'll teach her a lot about responsibility," she answered with a smile.

"Well, last night he was doing a back float in the bathroom sink," I exclaimed. "In a bubble bath!"

Mom let out a deep sigh and rubbed her temples.

"Brianna, Brianna, Brianna . . . ," she muttered in exhaustion. "What am I going to do with that child?"

"Mom, she didn't believe me when I told her Rover was dead. She loves that fish like it's her own baby! She's going to be traumatized when she finally figures out she cooked him in a bubble bath."

I remember when I had a goldfish at her age. His name was Mr. Fish-n-Chips.

All the kids in my class brought their pets to show-and-tell, so I wanted to do the same.

I put Mr. Fish-n-Chips in a box with holes in it so he could breathe, and carried him to school.

Well, you can imagine what I discovered when I opened up that box for show-and-tell!

"I know it's going to be sad when Brianna learns the truth. I wish there was another option," Mom said, shaking her head.

Suddenly her eyes lit up.

"I have an idea! And if we hurry, we can get there before they close at nine p.m.!"

I looked at the clock and back at her in confusion. It was 8:43 p.m.

Normally, she'd be nagging me to finish my homework and get ready for bed.

"I don't get it! WHERE are we going?" I asked.

"Hurry!" she exclaimed as she grabbed her coat. "I'll explain everything in the car on the way."

MOM, ABOUT TO TAKE ME ON
A MYSTERY ROAD TRIP!

We jumped into the car and she floored it.

"Um, MOM, can you . . . SLOW DOWN?!!"

"I can't! We only have ten minutes before they close!" she yelled back.

The rest of the ride was a blur.

Before I knew it, we were parked in the middle of an empty Pets-N-Stuff parking lot. As we were getting out of the car, we saw a store clerk locking the doors.

"Oh. No. They. Didn't!" Mom yelled. "We still have a good six minutes left to shop! They can't close early!"

She jumped out of the car and stormed up to the Pets-N-Stuff door. I scurried after her.

Inside, an employee was sweeping the floor. He saw us standing there but completely ignored us. Then he rolled his eyes and turned his back to us.

"HEY!!" Mom banged her fist on the glass door. "YOU DON'T CLOSE TILL NINE! WE STILL HAVE FIVE MINUTES TO SHOP! OPEN UP!!"

41

ME AND MY MOM, TRYING TO BREAK
INTO A CLOSED STORE!!

The dude looked totally annoyed. He muttered some stuff that I was probably glad I couldn't hear and kept sweeping.

So Mom just kept pounding on the glass door. I was praying that it wouldn't break and shatter into a million pieces! Finally, the guy dropped the broom, unlocked the door, and poked his head out, scowling angrily.

"When the doors are locked, that's a hint for customers to get lost!" he snapped at Mom. "We're closed, lady! Deal with it!"

He was about to slam the door shut, but Mom stuck her foot in the way.

"Listen here!" she growled, waving her finger in his face. "We have a dead goldfish emergency at home, so I am NOT in a very good mood! Now, YOU'RE going to let us in so we can buy a new one, because I am NOT doing another fish funeral! Do you have any idea how traumatic a fish funeral is for a child? WELL? DO YOU?!"

"N—no, ma'am!" the guy stuttered nervously, his eyes as big as saucers.

He must've thought we had just broken out of a mental hospital or something!

"That's right! You DON'T know!" Mom continued. "So let us in! Or so help me, I'll go straight to Pets-N-Stuff national headquarters to complain about how horrific your customer service is! Do I make myself clear, young man?"

"VERY clear, ma'am!" he said, with a fake smile plastered across his face. "Please come in!"

"Hmph!" Mom stuck her nose in the air and walked into the store like she owned the place. I scrambled after her.

I have to admit, it was kind of fun watching her tell off that jerk-of-a-clerk!

We searched all the aquariums for Rover's identical twin, but no luck.

Then, just as we were about to give up, I spotted a fish the exact same size and orangey color as Rover hiding behind a small castle.

ME AND THE NEW GOLDFISH,
GETTING TO KNOW EACH OTHER!

Mom and I were so happy to have finally found our fish that we gave each other a high five.

While she was at the checkout counter paying for the brand-new Rover, I noticed a poster for a contest to win dog food near the front door.

ENTER TODAY AND WIN A
FREE ONE-YEAR SUPPLY OF

# DOGGY DINER
## DOG FOOD!!

NO PURCHASE NECESSARY!
Just fill out your entry form and
deposit it in the box.

Of course I immediately thought of the Fuzzy Friends Animal Rescue Center, where Brandon volunteers! A free one-year supply of dog food could really help out the center. And, who knows, I might just win!

Any money saved on food expenses would mean additional dollars that Brandon could use to care for even MORE homeless animals. That would make him SO happy! A big smile spread across my face just thinking about him.

I suddenly realized just how much our friendship meant to me. So I decided to text him a huge apology as soon as I got back to the car.

I filled out the little card with Brandon's name and address, kissed it for good luck, and then dropped it into the big box with the rest of the entries.

I was standing at the front door, waiting for my mom, when I noticed a SUPERcute guy walk out of the shop next door, listening to his tunes. Only, it wasn't just ANY SUPERcute guy. . . .

IT WAS BRANDON?!!

And he had a PIZZA!

But it wasn't just ANY pizza!

It was a QUEASY CHEESY TAKEOUT pizza ☹!!

I gasped and stared in disbelief with my face pressed against the door.

Then I screamed, "NOOOOOOO!!!"

Only, I just said it inside my head, so no one else heard it but me.

As I watched Brandon disappear around the corner, I felt like my heart had dropped into my sneakers and splattered all over the floor.

Okay, NOW I was starting to worry that the rumor WAS true!

Which also meant I had to ask myself a very difficult and potentially heartbreaking QUESTION about that KISS. . . .

Were Chloe and Zoey going to be so ANGRY at Brandon that they'd THREATEN to give him a BEATDOWN like they did at the Sweetheart Dance back in February??!!!

OMG! That fiasco was CRAY-CRAY! Especially when Chloe totally lost it and went all Karate Kid in her fancy ball gown! Of course I was also DYING to know the answers to a few other questions. Had Brandon:

1. kissed me on a DARE just to get a free pizza, as MacKenzie had alleged?

2. kissed me only because he wanted to help raise money for charity to help the needy children of the world?

Or

3. kissed me because he considered me MORE than just a good friend?

Suddenly I felt SO confused!

It was quite obvious that I didn't know Brandon as well as I thought I did.

Anyway, by the time my mom and I finally made it back home, Brianna was fast asleep.

We tiptoed into Brianna's room and made the swap.

And as we were leaving, I could see the new Rover happily swimming around in circles.

Mission. Accomplished!!

By then I was so exhausted by the whole Brandon drama that I went straight to bed.

But I just lay awake, staring at the ceiling and trying to figure out what went wrong in our relationship.

Then I got up and started writing in my diary.

Suddenly it made perfect sense why Brandon had been so defensive on Thursday and seemingly eager to back off and give me some space.

It was probably his GUILTY conscience!

Or maybe he just wanted to start hanging out with MacKenzie.

Which is perfectly fine with me! MISS DIVA and MR. DARE totally deserve each other!!

Right now I'm so OVER Brandon!

I wouldn't care if he took a bite of his stupid pizza and CHOKED on a PEPPERONI!

I just want OFF this crazy emotional roller coaster!

☹!!

Brianna snuck into my room while I was sleeping.

"BOO!" she shouted into my ear, and giggled.

"Good morning, Brianna," I answered without flinching (after the hundredth time, it doesn't even scare me anymore). "Why don't you go somewhere and pick your nose so I can sleep?"

"Rover wanted to say hi!" she said, holding the fishbowl up to my face. "He finally woke up from his nap! See?"

The new Rover was STILL happily swimming around in circles. Thank goodness!

"And he still smells nice and clean from his bath!" she chirped. "You wanna sniff?"

"No! What I WANT is for you and Rover to get out of my room. Please!" I grumped, and threw my blanket over my head.

"We're gonna play dolls and watch TV. And then I'm gonna feed Rover a yummy breakfast!"

When Brianna said "breakfast," I assumed she'd be feeding him FISH FOOD! NOT . . .

PRINCESS SUGAR PLUM CEREAL!!

OMG! I was SO disgusted with Brianna!

Mom and I could be sitting in jail for practically breaking and entering a closed pet store.

All because Brianna didn't know how to take care of her stupid fish!

But one thing was clear! We needed to get poor Rover back to school before Brianna KILLED him. AGAIN!

Mom called Brianna's teacher to apologize and let her know that we had to replace the goldfish.

But apparently, not even the Rover that Brianna had brought home was the original Rover.

Her teacher explained that, unfortunately, other children before Brianna had also had similar "accidents."

Which meant the Rover we'd just bought was actually Rover the Ninth!

I was really shocked and surprised to hear that news.

Mom and I both agreed that Brianna was nowhere near ready for a real, live pet goldfish yet.

Although, I could always buy some of those Goldfish snack crackers and dump them in the fishbowl with a little bubble bath.

As long as they floated upside down on their backs (like the original Rover), Brianna would NEVER know the difference!

Anyway, since she has to return Rover to her classroom tomorrow, she's decided she wants to buy a pet fish with arms so it can play dolls and bake chocolate cupcakes with her.

I was like, "Sorry, Brianna! But fish DON'T have arms!"

But she said, "Uh-huh, they do! I saw one on the Internet and I'm already saving my allowance!" . . .

BRIANNA'S PET FISH WITH ARMS
(ALSO KNOWN AS A MERMAID)

Well, one thing is for sure!

If Brianna gives her NEW pet fish with arms a bubble bath and feeds her Princess Sugar Plum Cereal like she did with Rover, things could get a whole lot MESSIER really fast! I'm just sayin' . . . !!

With all the Rover drama, I completely forgot to mention the MOST important thing that happened today!!

I got frantic texts from both Chloe and Zoey about a crazy rumor they'd just heard about ME that involved Brandon, a pizza, and a kiss ☹!!

Of course I told them EVERYTHING. They both rushed over to my house and we talked for what seemed like hours.

Now I'm feeling a lot better. Maybe my life isn't a bottomless pit of despair after all!

Chloe and Zoey are the BEST friends EVER!! I don't know what I'd do without them! ☹!!

It was another typical day in gym class. The exercises were pointless, the CCP kids were slacking off, and the gym teacher was yelling at them.

I was still fuming about the Brandon situation.

"I CAN'T believe it! It's like I've been bought and sold for a cruddy pizza!" I ranted.

Since it was still a bit too chilly to play tennis outside, we practiced inside by hitting tennis balls against the gym wall.

It was actually very therapeutic for me since I needed something to help burn off all the negative energy I had pent up inside.

To put it bluntly, I was so TICKED OFF, I wanted to SMACK something!

But on a more positive note, my BFFs and I looked SUPERcute in our chic tennis outfits. . . .

ME AND MY BFFS, CHATTING
AND HITTING TENNIS BALLS IN
OUR CUTE-N-CHIC OUTFITS!

"I thought Brandon was a really nice guy. But I didn't really know him at all!" I fumed.

"Nikki, just calm down!" Zoey said. "I know it looks like the rumor might be true. But maybe Brandon bought the pizza with his allowance?"

"Really? What IDIOT would spend a dime on a cruddy Queasy Cheesy pizza?" I shot back.

"A really HUNGRY idiot?" Chloe answered. "I got a great deal on a shrimp pizza there last week."

"But he said he owes me an apology, so that must mean the rumor is true! And WHY did he just walk away when I was trying to talk to him?" I asked.

"I'm pretty sure it was probably because you were screaming at him about RUINING your life," Zoey replied. "But I could be wrong."

"Maybe he walked away to go look for a rock. You DID tell him to go SLITHER back under a rock, right?" Chloe quipped.

"Okay, I'll admit it. That part was MY fault! I just wish I knew for sure if all the stuff MacKenzie said about a DARE is true!" I said, and whacked my ball even harder. "Because now I'll NEVER know if my very first kiss was just a big JOKE! And it's DRIVING. ME. CRAZY!!!"

I slammed my tennis ball in anger, and we barely managed to duck as it ricocheted off the wall and shot across the gym at what seemed like a hundred miles an hour.

Chloe raised an eyebrow at me. "CRAZY is an understatement! Nikki, you're BEATING your poor tennis ball like it owes you money!" she snarked.

"Sorry!" I muttered.

Suddenly Zoey's eyes lit up. "Listen up, guys! I have an idea! And yes, I know it's crazy! But why don't we just call Queasy Cheesy and ask them to send us a copy of Brandon's receipt?! Then we can see if he personally paid for the pizza or if someone bought it for him because of a dare like MacKenzie said."

"Sorry, Zoey, but Queasy Cheesy would NEVER send a customer receipt to a bunch of silly, nosy girls like US!" I grumbled.

"I bet they would if they thought the silly, nosy girls were CUSTOMERS!" Chloe squealed as she did jazz hands. "All we have to do is pretend to be BRANDON!"

"OMG! That would totally work," Zoey agreed excitedly. "We'll call and say he lost his receipt and needs a new copy. We can ask them to text a copy to us."

"Are you guys NUTS?!" I practically screamed at my BFFs. "We can't pretend to be Brandon! Aren't there laws against that kind of thing?!"

That's when Chloe and Zoey gave each other "the look."

ME, VERY SUSPICIOUS THAT
CHLOE AND ZOEY ARE PLOTTING
TO BAMBOOZLE ME!

And I knew from experience that "the look" meant
they were going to try to SWEET-TALK me into
doing something I DIDN'T want to do!

64

I absolutely HATE being BAMBOOZLED ☹!!

"Okay, Nikki. Just forget about it!" Zoey
said, suddenly looking extremely bored as she
bounced her tennis ball on her racket. *BOUNCE.*
*BOUNCE. BOUNCE. BOUNCE.* "If you want to
live your life and then DIE not ever knowing
if your first kiss was possibly TRUE LOVE,
go right ahead!"

Chloe yawned and picked at her nails. "Well, Nikki,
the good news is that when you're old and lonely,
you can always spend your last days pondering
whether or not Brandon bought his pizza with
cash or won it from a dare. Cash or dare. Cash or
dare. Cash or dare. Cash or—"

"Okay, guys! STOP IT!! Just STOP!"
I yelled at them.

Unfortunately, their BAMBOOZLING was
working.

As usual.

"You've made your point," I continued. "This thing could haunt me for the rest of my life. I DO want to know the truth. But I DON'T want to end up in jail trying to find out. And most important, I don't want to give MacKenzie the satisfaction of RUINING my first kiss! So what I'm trying to say is that I'd really appreciate your help on this, guys."

We happily did a three-way fist bump to show our solidarity as BFFs and our commitment to uncovering the truth behind the rumor.

"Okay, my biggest worry is that Queasy Cheesy would never believe us," I explained. "WHY would Brandon suddenly need an emergency copy of an old pizza receipt from two days ago?!"

"Well, I dunno. Maybe he needs it for, um . . . tax purposes?" Zoey said.

"Tax purposes?! Hmm, that DOES sound really legit," I said, tapping my chin, deep in thought. "You know what, Zoey?! I think it just might work!"

"I agree! It's brilliant! Pure genius!" Chloe said excitedly. "Um, what does 'for tax purposes' mean?"

"Actually, I don't have the slightest idea." Zoey shrugged. "But whenever my parents lose a receipt or important papers, people always send them new copies whenever they say it's for tax purposes."

"Yeah, I've heard my parents use that excuse too," I agreed. "And it works like a charm!"

"Wow! I think I'm going to try that the next time I bomb on a test!" Chloe snickered. "I'll just tell my teacher I lost the test paper with the bad grade and request a new test for tax purposes. Getting a do-over on a test for tax purposes could really boost my grades."

"Sorry, Chloe, but I don't think it'll fix bad grades." Zoey giggled.

"Hey, it wouldn't hurt to try!" Chloe grinned.

"Anyway, I think we should make the call from the library phone so that it appears more official. Then Queasy Cheesy won't be as quick to blow us off since we're not adults," Zoey explained.

"Why don't we call during lunch tomorrow?" I suggested. "Hardly anyone hangs out in the library during lunch on Tuesdays."

Chloe insisted on being the one to make the call as Brandon. She reasoned that since she'd read the most teen novels with hunky guys in them, she could really "get inside their heads."

Whatever that means!

We also decided to have the receipt texted to Zoey's cell phone since it has better reception in the library than Chloe's and mine.

My assignment is to pick up three library shelving assistant passes from the school office so we can leave the cafeteria during lunch to hang out in the library.

And yes! I feel a little guilty about getting LSA passes to work in the library when we don't actually plan on shelving any books.

But making that phone call to Queasy Cheesy and getting to the bottom of all the recent drama is a WAY more important task as far as I'm concerned.

Because honestly, I just don't know if I can trust Brandon anymore.

And the fact that our friendship is ending like this is absolute TORTURE!!

☹!!

I've been a nervous wreck all morning! Very soon I'll know if that rumor MacKenzie has been spreading about Brandon is true.

I also had this really uneasy feeling, like I was forgetting to do something SUPERimportant.

As soon as gym class was over, Chloe, Zoey, and I rushed to the cafeteria and quickly snarfed down our lunches.

We were about to dump our trays and head for the library when I FINALLY remembered what I'd forgotten!

Our LSA passes to the library!!! Oh, CRUD ☹!!

Unfortunately, we had to either cancel our secret plan or risk an after-school detention by SNEAKING to the library without any passes.

Although I had messed things up, Chloe and Zoey STILL insisted on making that phone call.

But the difficult task of sneaking out of the cafeteria suddenly became IMPOSSIBLE when . . .

PRINCIPAL WINSTON PARKED HIS BUTT RIGHT AT OUR TABLE AND THEN JUST STOOD THERE, LIKE, FOREVER ☹!!

Of course we didn't dare make any moves. We didn't want to RUIN our rep as quiet, studious, rule-abiding dorks.

I bet Winston would NEVER guess we regularly hung out in the janitor's closet, which was strictly off-limits to students.

Hey! It was our LITTLE secret ☺!

When I texted this to Chloe and Zoey, they couldn't stop giggling. Chloe texted back that our BIG secret was that we made prank calls from the library phone ☺! And Zoey texted that our HUMONGOUS secret was that we'd snuck into the boys' locker room ☺!

Lucky for us, Winston finally wandered over to the other side of the cafeteria to eyeball a table of football players who were having a contest to see who could shove the most mac and cheese up their nose.

We quickly dumped our trays and snuck out the door . . . behind a very smelly garbage can.

MY BFFS AND ME, VERY STEALTHILY
SNEAKING TO THE LIBRARY BEHIND
A VERY SMELLY GARBAGE CAN!

Since we had been delayed by Principal Winston, by the time we made it to the library we had less than three minutes to make our phone call and get to class.

We excitedly huddled around the phone as Chloe dialed the number.

"What's up, bro! Is this Queasy Cheesy? Cool! Yo, my name is Brandon and I was in there a few days ago snagging a pizza and, dude, I lost my receipt. And I, like, really need that receipt for, um . . . tax purposes. . . . Huh? I said tax purposes! . . . No, NOT tacks porpoises. Hey, bro, this has nothing to do with thumbtacks or those big fish that look like dolphins, okay? I said TAX! PURPOSES! . . . Yeah, that's it! Cool! . . . Do I remember what I ordered? Of course I do! Not all guys are stupid. We can remember lots of stuff. I ordered . . . um . . . ! Could you hold on a second? I have to . . . burp? It's a guy thing, ya know?"

Zoey and I both cringed.

74

Chloe put her hand over the receiver and whispered frantically, "Nikki, he wants to know what my order was! Do you know what Brandon ordered?"

"Actually, Chloe, I'm not sure what his order was!" I whisper-shouted. "I never saw him actually eating it. But whatever it was, it was in the pizza box he was carrying. I'm guessing it was probably a large pizza. Oh, I almost forgot, he also had a soda bottle on top of the pizza box."

Chloe continued into the phone. "Well, DUDE! It's like this. Actually, I'm not sure what I ordered since I never saw myself eating it. But whatever it was, it was in the pizza box I was carrying! I'm guessing it was probably a large pizza. And I drank a soda that was on top of my pizza box. Did you get all that, bro?"

Zoey and I both did a giant eye roll.

I was worried sick that at some point the Queasy Cheesy guy was going to assume Chloe was a prank call and just hang up on her.

Chloe went on. "So you want to know the date and time? Um, of course I know that. But hold on, I have to go spit. Most football players spit, and I play a lot of football, fo' sure! Be right back!"

It was like Chloe had lost her mind. Why was she saying all that crazy stuff?!

"Nikki, he wants the date and time!" Chloe whispered nervously.

"Um, okay. Brianna accidentally killed her fish on Friday, and we picked up a new one Saturday night. I saw Brandon from the Pets-N-Stuff door a little after nine p.m. But please! You don't have to tell him every little detail since it's none of his business."

Chloe cleared her throat. "Okay, listen up, dude. My best friend's little sister killed her fish on Friday and my friend picked up a new one Saturday night. Then I saw um . . . myself from the Pets-N-Stuff door a little after nine p.m. But I don't have to tell you every little detail since it's none of your business. Got that, bro? Great! . . . Okay, I'll hold."

Zoey and I shook our heads in disbelief.

My fear was that Chloe had probably been placed on hold so that the manager could call the FBI to report a suspicious caller trying to gain access to private customer info to commit identity theft or something.

The call would be traced to us in the school library and a SWAT team of twenty-nine officers would come crashing through the windows to take us into custody.

Then after what seemed like forever . . .

"OMG! You actually found the receipt and are going to send it! SQUEEEE!" Chloe squealed.

Then, assuming her phony identity, she quickly added, "WHOA! I don't know what came over me. THAT was weird! Sorry, dude. What I actually meant to say was, you found my receipt and will text it to me?! That's cool, bro, very cool!"

CHLOE, ZOEY, AND ME, HAPPY AND RELIEVED
THAT QUEASY CHEESY AGREED
TO SEND THE RECEIPT!

Chloe gave the guy Zoey's phone number and then continued. "Thanks a lot, dude! I love you, bro! To infinity and beyond! Later!"

Then she hung up the phone and gushed, "We did it! He's texting the receipt to Zoey right now!"

I couldn't believe that Chloe had actually pulled it off.

She was absolutely HORRIBLE and terribly HILARIOUS, all at the same time.

We were SO happy that we did a group hug ☺!!!

I consider myself really lucky to have great BFFs like Chloe and Zoey.

We waited nervously for the text to arrive, and when it finally did, Zoey handed her cell phone to me.

My hands were practically shaking as I read over Brandon's receipt. . . .

## QUEASY CHEESY
## TAKEOUT

### THE WORLD'S BEST PIZZA
### SATURDAY, APRIL 5  9:04 P.M.

**\*\*RECEIPT\*\***

| | |
|---|---|
| 1 LARGE MEAT LOVERS PIZZA | $9.99 |
| 1 COLA DRINK | $1.21 |
| TAX & DEPOSIT | $0.80 |
| TOTAL | $12.00 |
| CASH | $0.00 |
| QC GIFT CARD | $12.00 |
| CHANGE DUE | $0.00 |

**\*\*THANK YOU!\*\***

I blinked in shock and disbelief and read the receipt over several times.

Brandon had NOT purchased the pizza from Queasy Cheesy with cash ☹!!!

Which meant that MacKenzie WAS telling the truth!

It had been paid for with a gift card! A gift card that, according to MacKenzie, had been won from a DARE that involved ME!

That little receipt told me a lot more than just the type of pizza Brandon had ordered.

It revealed that . . .

The rumor was TRUE!!

MacKenzie was RIGHT!!

Brandon was NOT MY FRIEND!!

And my very first kiss was a complete and utter SHAM!!

# AAAAAAAAAAHHH!!
(That was me screaming!!!)

!!

## WEDNESDAY, APRIL 9

Today I had a meeting with Mr. Zimmerman, the adviser of our school newspaper, about the advice column I secretly write, Just Ask Miss Know-It-All.

Since my week has been a complete nightmare, I half expected him to FIRE me on the spot!

I nervously poked my head into his office. "Hi, Mr. Zimmerman, you wanted to see—"

"NO! I don't want any!" he yelled. "NOW GET OUT OF MY OFFICE!!"

"I'm SO sorry!" I gasped, and turned to leave.

"Wait a minute, Nikki! YOU can come in! But NOT those kids who smell like Doritos and video games," he muttered.

Mr. Zimmerman is actually a nice teacher! He's just VERY . . . um, WEIRD!

It took me a while to get used to his high-strung personality and the fact that he spirals through at least five different moods daily. Which means I never quite know which one I'm going to have to deal with.

I slowly peeked inside his office again to find him slumped over his desk with sunglasses on.

His office was messy, with stacks of paper piled everywhere.

He gestured for me to have a seat, so I timidly walked over and sat down.

"PLEASE! DON'T WALK SO LOUDLY!! I HAVE A SPLITTING HEADACHE!" he grumbled.

"I—I'm really sorry!" I stammered. "I didn't know!"

"Yes, you DID! I just TOLD you a few seconds ago. I said please don't walk so loudly, I have a splitting headache. Don't you remember?!"

ME, TRYING TO APOLOGIZE TO
MR. ZIMMERMAN FOR ~~TALKING~~
WALKING TOO LOUDLY!

"Um, okay then," I said, and quickly changed the subject. "Anyway, I'm here because you wanted to see me about my Miss Know-It-All column. I hope everything is okay?"

"Actually, your advice column is more popular than ever! You're on your way to becoming the next Oprah! Keep up the good work!"

Then he explained that to make it easier to answer the large volume of mail I was receiving, he had arranged for the computer club to design a Miss Know-It-All website.

So now students needing advice can either leave a handwritten letter in one of my help boxes located around the school or e-mail me!

Thanks to Mr. Zimmerman, I have my very own Miss Know-It-All website.

This is actually great news. Although, it's about time SOMETHING went right, for once in my life.

**Just Ask... MISS KNOW-IT-ALL!**

## MY BRAND-NEW
## MISS KNOW-IT-ALL WEBSITE ☺!

Mr. Zimmerman said that Lauren, his intern, would also scan the handwritten letters and e-mail them to me to be stored on the website.

This will make my job A LOT easier!

Then he reached into his pocket and handed me a crumpled-up Post-it note.

"Now, here's the info for your site. Your user ID is on the second line, and your password is on the third line."

```
TO-DO LIST:
▚▞▚▞▚▞▚▞▚▞▚▞▚▞▚▞▚▞▚▞▚

1 Buy milk

2 Yoga class at 7 pm
```

"This is highly sensitive information! So guard it with your life! And if you don't, you're automatically FIRED!" he said solemnly.

"FIRED?!" I gulped. "Really?!"

"Yes, really! It took me almost four hours to set up that user ID and password! And now I can't find my to-do list. It'll be easier and less time-consuming for me to just FIRE you than spend another four hours setting up new ones. So please! Don't mess this up!"

I wanted to mention that it looked to me like my user ID and password WERE his to-do list.

But since Mr. Zimmerman was already having a rough day with his headache and all, I didn't want to risk upsetting him again.

So I just smiled, thanked him, and stuck the note in my pocket.

Then, using my new user ID and password, we logged into the website and he explained how everything worked.

I can't wait to start answering letters using the new site. Working on my advice column is going to be more fun than ever!

"Is there anything else?" he finally asked, glancing at his Ninja Turtles clock on the wall.

"No, I don't think so," I answered. "But I want to thank you again for my new Miss Know-It-All site!"

"You're very welcome!" Mr. Zimmerman said, adjusting his sunglasses and slumping back down in his chair. "NOW GET OUT OF MY OFFICE!! I've wasted enough time talking to you! And I STILL have to find my missing to-do list!"

Anyway, after our meeting, I was absolutely certain about ONE thing!

The man is more NUTTY than a Reese's Peanut Butter Cup ☹!!

But you gotta love him ☺!!

Anyway, I'm really happy that my advice column is going so well, even though the rest of my life is in SHAMBLES.

OMG! I just got the most brilliant idea!

I should write a letter to Miss Know-It-All!

Then maybe I'll give MYSELF great advice on how I can solve all my OWN personal problems!

☺!!

NOTE TO SELF:

**EXTREMELY IMPORTANT INFO!!**

Miss Know-It-All advice column website:

User ID: 1Buymilk

Password: 2Yogaclassat7pm

Remember to guard this with your life!!

Or you're AUTOMATICALLY FIRED!!

☹!!

I arrived at school early to work on my Miss Know-It-All advice column. It was the perfect distraction from all the drama I've been dealing with lately.

I just hoped I wouldn't run into you-know-who. Since our big fight last week, he and I have basically ignored each other.

When I walked into the newspaper office, the first thing I saw was a group of kids laughing hysterically at a video they were watching on a cell phone.

Apparently, the guy showing it had gotten it from a girl who'd recorded a classmate.

Since I love funny videos as much as the next kid, I decided to stop and check it out.

OMG!! It was so SHOCKING, I almost lost the oatmeal I ate for breakfast! It was a video of . . .

MACKENZIE HOLLISTER,
HAVING A MELTDOWN ABOUT THAT
STINK BUG IN HER HAIR!!

There she was in our French class, screaming, jumping up and down, and shaking her head like she'd lost her mind.

And get this! Someone had added MUSIC to the video. So it looked like she was doing that wacky dance that was all the rage for a hot minute called the Harlem Shake!

It was really painful to watch ☹! But I did watch. Because it was HILARIOUS ☺!!

If/when MacKenzie finds out kids are passing around that AWFUL video of her, she's going to have an EPIC meltdown.

And it'll be ten times WORSE than the one she had over that stupid stink bug.

I have to admit, that video is just . . . CRUEL!!

Although MacKenzie is NOT my favorite person, I feel really, really SORRY for her ☹!

NOT 😊!!

Hey, I'm STILL traumatized from the time she took that video of me dancing and singing onstage with Brianna at Queasy Cheesy.

And then POSTED IT ON YOUTUBE 😟!!

A VERY EMBARRASSING VIDEO OF
ME DANCING AND SINGING ONSTAGE
WITH MY LITTLE SISTER!

Maybe now MacKenzie will know what it feels like to be so utterly HUMILIATED that all you want to do is dig a very deep HOLE . . .

CRAWL into it . . .

And DIE!! ☹!!

I really hope this experience teaches her a valuable lesson.

But she can consider herself LUCKY!

At least no one has put HER video on the INTERNET for millions of people to watch.

YET!!

☺!!

# FRIDAY, APRIL 11

Dear Nikki,

Sorry, but I think you've just LOST something very IMPORTANT 🙂!

(Well, other than your CUTE but ADORKABLE crush, Brandon! And maybe your PRIDE!!)

Hmm . . . now, WHAT could it be?!!

Your backpack? Nope!

Your geometry textbook? Nope!

Your French homework? Nope!

How about something from that super-tacky wardrobe of yours?

I WISH!! The world would be a much better place without your HIDEOUS polyester pants 🙁!!

And where did you get those cheapo shoes?!
Let me guess. They were the FREE prize in
your McDonald's Happy Meal?!

Anyway, let me start by explaining exactly
how I got my hot little hands on YOUR most
cherished TREASURE.

Like always, I got up at exactly 6:15 a.m.,
showered, and did ten minutes of yoga.

Then I had a continental breakfast with
freshly squeezed orange juice, half a bagel
with goat cheese, and a green smoothie,
all served on a silver tray by my maid,
Olga, right in my bedroom.

BTW, green smoothies are vital in helping
me maintain my FLAWLESS complexion. Along
with weekly visits to the U-PAY WE-SPRAY
tanning salon.

Then I had to decide which of my FAB designer
looks I was going to ROCK in school today.....

FRESH-N-FIERCE FASHIONISTA?!

98

BOHO BRAINS-N-BEAUTY?!

OR . . . SWEET CHIC-N-SASSY?!

100

Yes, I know! As always, I looked super GLAMFABULOUS in ALL my ensembles!

But after trying on all three and consulting with my personal stylist via Skype (she's currently on tour with Taylor Swift), I chose Sweet Chic-n-Sassy.

Since Daddy was in Europe (again!) and Mommy had an extra-early appointment at the spa for a facial, our driver, Nelson, dropped me off at school in our black limo.

Which, BTW, does NOT have a six-foot-long plastic ROACH thingy on top of it!!

Like SOME people I know.

Seriously! How HUMILIATING is that?!

Sorry, but if I had to ride around in a JALOPY with a giant INSECT on top of it . . .

OMG! I CAN'T EVEN . . . !!!

I'd BLINDFOLD myself, strike a FIERCE POSE, and PAY Nelson to RUN OVER me with my LIMO.

ME, BLINDFOLDED, GETTING
RUN OVER BY MY LIMO

I'd put a PAPER BAG over my head and THROW myself into the Grand Canyon!!

ME, THROWING MYSELF INTO
THE GRAND CANYON!!

Or I'd smear DOUBLE CHEESEBURGERS all over my body and then JUMP into the SHARK TANK at Sea World!!

ME, ABOUT TO JUMP INTO
THE SHARK TANK AT SEA WORLD!!

Actually, I'm just kidding, hon 😊!!

That GINORMOUS plastic roach is apparently an important member of your family. Because YOUR little sister told MY little sister that his name is MAX and he's the family PET!

Nikki, you obviously have an extremely WEIRD family!! I feel SO sorry for MAX!

Anyway, as I was saying, after Nelson dropped me off at school I headed straight to my locker to put on more lip gloss and—

OOPSIE! Someone is coming down the hall!

So, unfortunately, I have to stop writing now.

And, Nikki, you'd NEVER guess who that "someone" is!!

It's YOU, hon 😊! You and your silly friends, Chloe and Zoey, are giggling and scampering

down the hall like a pack of socially
challenged CHIPMUNKS!

You obviously have no idea that your precious
little DIARY is missing!! Yes! I said DIARY!!

I can't wait to see you have a BIG FAT HISSY FIT
when you finally realize it's gone!

But for now I'll just hide it in my new
Verna Bradshaw designer handbag that I
bought (on sale for 20% off!) at the mall
yesterday.

Next period I plan to get a bathroom pass
from our French teacher. And while you're
busily conjugating verbs, I'll be READING
your diary ☺!

# TOODLES!

MacKenzie ♥

Dear Nikki,

I have no idea why you spend hours and hours writing in this stupid little diary of yours.

But let me guess! It's because you seriously need to GET A LIFE!

When I want to share my life experiences or vent about something, I just talk to Mommy and Daddy.

Of course, sometimes Mommy is super busy being a socialite and doing charity work.

And sometimes Daddy is super busy building his multimillion-dollar business empire.

But when my very dedicated parents can't spend quality time with me (which I have to admit happens far too frequently these days), I can always rely on Dr. Hadley, my therapist.

He will listen to me patiently for an ENTIRE hour as long as Daddy pays him $480 a session. AND I get to go TWICE a week if I want to!! How COOL is that?! I'm a VERY lucky girl ☺! But please don't be jealous of me, okay?

I feel really SORRY for you, Nikki, because ALL you have for emotional support are your very WEIRD parents. And this STUPID little diary.

And nobody else cares about you! Except maybe your bratty little sister, Brianna. Oh, and Chloe and Zoey. And probably Marcy, Violet, and Jenny. Of course, there's also Theo and Marcus.

But Brandon? Rumor has it that he's so OVER you ☺! Sorry, hon, but your BOO has moved on.

My point is that YOU have no REAL friends WHATSOEVER!

And you're insanely JEALOUS that the CCPs practically WORSHIP the ground I walk on!!

Anyway, I need to make one thing perfectly clear:

# I DID NOT STEAL YOUR DIARY!

I have way too much integrity to stoop that low. Besides, Daddy would buy me an entire DIARY FACTORY in some poor third-world country if I really wanted one! Just sayin'.

He mostly gives me everything I want, especially if I throw a temper tantrum about it. And Mommy says I'm an even bigger DRAMA QUEEN than SHE is ☺! They both SO adore me!

So, yesterday I was on my way to my locker to freshen up my lip gloss. My stylist says you can NEVER wear too much lip gloss!

YOU had just rushed off to class, when I witnessed a very CATASTROPHIC event. . . .

109

ME, IN TOTAL SHOCK THAT YOUR LOCKER DOOR <u>DIDN'T</u> CLOSE DUE TO YOUR VERY UGLY PUKE-COLORED COAT!!

That coat of yours was so HIDEOUS that it gave me hives. I seriously contemplated dialing 911 for an ambulance.

But not for ME! I wanted them to transport your puke-colored coat to the city DUMP. And then BURN it as a public health hazard.

And YES, Nikki, I sincerely did try to alert you to the fact that your coat sleeve was stuck in your locker door.

But due to my severe allergic reaction to your coat, all I could muster was a weak and very hoarse whisper that you apparently didn't hear.

Of course, ALL of this was totally YOUR fault! WHY any rational HUMAN BEING would wear a PUKE-COLORED coat to school is beyond explanation, logic, and reason!!

Seriously, I CAN'T EVEN . . . !!!

Anyway, by the time I started to recover from the HORROR I'd just experienced, you had already hopped happily down the hall like some CLUELESS little bunny and disappeared.

That's when I became so worried about your open locker that I went into a full-blown PANIC ATTACK!!

What if someone stole your textbooks? Our school would suffer a financial loss!

What if someone stole your house keys? Your family's safety would be at risk!

What if someone stole your coat? They'd leave it in the woods so that a pregnant stray cat could have her kittens on it!

So, Nikki, in spite of the fact that I basically HATE YOUR GUTS (just kidding, hon ☺!), I decided to do the responsible thing and take measures to protect your most valuable and treasured personal possession.

ME, HEROICALLY CONFISCATING YOUR
DIARY BEFORE IT COULD GET STOLEN
AND READ BY THE ENTIRE SCHOOL!!

As you can see, I did not STEAL your diary!! Actually, you should THANK ME for what I did! Because otherwise, the pages containing your deepest, darkest secrets would be plastered all over the hallways by now.

I had every intention of returning your diary to you before social studies. But I barely got to class on time since I had to stop by the girls' bathroom to brush my hair.

And then I planned to give it back to you after gym class. But our gym teacher made me run three extra laps for talking to Jessica about your disgusting puke-colored coat during exercises.

And lastly, I was going to give it to you in bio. But I was preoccupied FLIRTING with BRANDON, while you watched and pretended that you WEREN'T insanely jealous ☺!

So at the end of the day I was FORCED to take your diary home with me for safekeeping!

To be very honest, Nikki, I've never liked you because I didn't really know you! And I'm guessing that you probably don't like me because you don't really know me.

So the fact that I'm reading your diary is actually a GOOD thing! I'm learning about your hopes, dreams, and fears, and all your deepest, darkest secrets.

And so that YOU can get to know ME better, I'm going to write some entries in your diary about me and my life!

I'll also DRAW in your diary so that you can see what a fabulously talented artist I am.

But please! Don't believe for one minute that you are actually as pretty as I am sketching you on these pages. I refuse to draw ugly people because they literally make me nauseous!

Anyway, Nikki, I really hope you enjoy reading . . .

# THE MACKENZIE DIARIES:
## TALES FROM A NOT-SO-DORKY DRAMA QUEEN

WELCOME TO MY WORLD, HON!!!

TOODLES!

MacKenzie

# SUNDAY, APRIL 13

Dear Nikki,

Today was so . . . totally FREAKY! Why?

Because I had a full-blown FASHION EMERGENCY!

OMG! I got a little dizzy and my palms actually started to sweat. EWW!!

My fashion stylist (who, BTW, is now on tour with Ariana Grande) says one should NEVER sweat! One should just . . . GLOW!

Anyway, it was vital that I rush out to the mall to find the PERFECT blouse to wear to school on Monday.

It needed to be:

Cute, but not too immature.

Classy, but not too boring.

Bold, but not too tacky.

Trendy, but not too faddish.

Finally, after shopping for what seemed like FOREVER, I found not one, not two, but THREE fabulous designer blouses!

And since I couldn't make up my mind which one I loved best, I decided to buy all THREE of them for only $689.32!

WHY?! Because I COULD!!

Yay ME ☺!!

Please don't HATE me because I'm rich!!

Then I rushed home and locked myself in my bedroom.

I had to make the very difficult decision of which blouse would best complement ~~your~~ MY diary!!

ME, TRYING TO DECIDE WHICH
FABULOUS BLOUSE BEST MATCHES
~~YOUR~~ MY DIARY!

However, the last thing I needed was for
some CRAZY girl at school to SEE me with

HER DIARY and accuse me of STEALING it!

Of course, initially no one would believe her because of my reputation for being a very kind and honest individual.

But if she told Principal Winston, there was a chance I could get BUSTED with it in my purse.

Which would mean an automatic suspension from WCD!!

And what if I was forced to attend a PUBLIC school?! Just like the ones I see on television?!

EWW ☹!!

Was this diary worth ALL that?!

I took a long, hard look at myself in the mirror and decided right then and there to do the ONLY thing that made sense.

ME, VERY INGENIOUSLY COVERING THE DIARY WITH FABRIC SO NO ONE WILL RECOGNIZE IT!!

YES! I know! I'm a BEAUTIFUL GENIUS ☺!!

It took me TWO whole hours to cover the diary with the leopard-print fabric from my brand-new designer blouse.

And when I finally finished, I was totally blown away by how FANTASTIC it looked.

The entire experience was so exciting and inspiring that I actually started to ~~sweat~~ GLOW!

That's when I rushed right back to the mall (thank goodness it hadn't closed yet!) and purchased another designer blouse, black leather pants, boots, and sunglasses.

Because tomorrow I plan to show off ~~your~~ MY new diary to EVERYONE at school!

YAY ME!! ☺!

Anyway, even though your diary only covered nine days in April, one thing is abundantly clear, Nikki. . . .

## YOU ARE
## ONE. SICK. LITTLE. COOKIE!!

Seriously, I can't believe I wasted hours of
my life reading all this whiny, fabricated
garbage.

Everything you wrote was like, "MacKenzie did THIS to me!" and "MacKenzie did THAT to me!" as if I'M the dysfunctional one!

Are you for real?! #Girlbye!

You are DELUSIONAL if you think you're the victim here!

Just face the truth!

You've been INSANELY JEALOUS of me from day one and are OBSESSED with trying to RUIN my life!

Brandon and I would be an item by now if you hadn't made him feel SORRY for you with all your "CUTE-N-DORKY" little antics.

You are BEYOND evil, Nikki Maxwell!

And you LIE so much, you should seriously consider a career in politics!

I think YOU need my therapist, Dr. Hadley, WAY more than I do!

I realize all the stuff I'm saying to you may sound cold, cruel, and mean. But I'm just being totally HONEST with you, Nikki.

Sorry I'm NOT sorry ☺!!

# TOODLES!

MacKenzie ♡

# MONDAY, APRIL 14

Dear Nikki,

Today was a super EXCITING day for me!

How was YOUR day, hon?

NOT very good? I thought so!

Especially after I saw you MOPING around school like a sad little puppy with your pathetic BFFs, Chloe and Zoey, trailing behind you. You guys looked really worried and appeared to be searching for something.

I wonder what?!

But enough about YOU! Let's talk about ME ☺!!

Didn't you just LOVE the brand-new designer outfit that I wore to school today?

It actually matched ~~your~~ MY diary!!

ME, KILLIN' IT IN MY NEW OUTFIT
WITH MATCHING DIARY!!

I think my new leopard-print cover looks ten times better than YOUR tacky blue-jean cover.

And that cute little pocket was SO immature!

Anyway, Nikki, when you and your BFFs walked up to your locker, I was standing just inches away from you, writing in ~~your~~ MY diary!

OMG! It was SURREAL!

But because I am a very compassionate person and you were obviously super upset about something, I asked you if anything was wrong.

"Excuse me, Nikki, but WHY are you throwing your JUNK all over the hallway? This is NOT your bedroom! WHAT is WRONG with you?!" I asked sweetly.

"Sorry, Mackenzie. We'll clean up my stuff in a minute," you said, rolling your sad eyes at me. "But right now we're busy looking for something really important, okay?"

ME, WATCHING YOU DESPERATELY
SEARCH FOR YOUR LOST DIARY!!

"Oh, really? Maybe I can help you find it. So, what did you lose, Nikki?" I asked, trying my best to be helpful.

That's when you, Chloe, and Zoey nervously glanced at each other and started whispering.

"So now it's a big secret?!" I asked, getting a little impatient. "Well . . . WHAT did you lose?!"

Then the three of you answered at exactly the same time. . . .

"Homework!" said Zoey.

"Sweater!" said Chloe.

"Cell phone!" you said.

"Wait a minute!" I exclaimed, totally confused. "WHAT exactly did you lose?!"

"Sweater!" said Zoey.

"Cell phone!" said Chloe.

"Homework!" you said.

You guys were obviously LYING to me, but I just played along with your little charade.

"So you lost homework, a sweater, AND a cell phone?!" I asked suspiciously.

Chloe and Zoey answered "No!" at the exact same time that you answered "Yes!"

Then Chloe and Zoey changed THEIR answer to "Yes!" at the same exact time that you changed YOUR answer to "No!"

And get this! THEN you all gave each other dirty looks and started whispering again. But I just played right along.

"Listen, you idiots!" I said impatiently. "I was going to offer to help you FIND whatever it is that you lost! But since you obviously don't know WHAT you're looking for, I won't bother!"

"MacKenzie, thanks. But please, just mind your OWN business!" Chloe said all snotty-like.

"Yeah, we GOT this!" Zoey added, glaring at me.

Sorry, but I couldn't resist it any longer.

"Fine! Then I WILL just mind my OWN business! I just hope you didn't lose your stupid little diary, Nikki! Because if it ever gets into the wrong hands, all your DIRTY little secrets will get out and this entire school will know what a big PHONY you are! Especially Brandon!"

OMG, Nikki! When I said the "D" word—DIARY—you looked like you'd just seen a ghost!! I really wish you could have seen your face! It was PRICELESS!!

The three of you just stared at me in complete shock with your mouths dangling open.

I wanted to pull out my cell phone and take a snapshot of you guys.

And then post it at:
#YouHaveNoIdeaHowStupidYouLookRightNow.

Anyway, you and your BFFs completely TRASHED your locker!

But you STILL didn't find your diary,
did you?!

# POOR BABY ☺!!

Well, I better get to class!

I completely lost track of time, and the
bell just rang.

I have to admit, this diary stuff is starting
to get kind of addicting!

# TOODLES!

MacKenzie♡

# TUESDAY, APRIL 15

Dear Nikki,

I'm having a HORRIBLE day today!! And it's all YOUR fault ☹!!

Today at lunch I was completely torn between the tofu salad and the tofu burger since I am very particular about what I eat.

I finally decided on the teriyaki tofu salad with honey ginger dressing and a chilled bottle of Mountain's Peak spring water. WHY? Because the tofu burger had a huge fly buzzing around it. EWW ☹!

Anyway, just as I was about to sit down at the CCP table, I saw all my friends laughing hysterically at a video of some stupid girl freaking out because she had a bug in her hair.

I was going to watch it and laugh too.
Until I realized SHE was ME!!

ME, IN SHOCK THAT MY FRIENDS
ARE LAUGHING AT ME!!

Suddenly my stomach started to feel very sick and QUEASY. Not from the video, but from the flashback to that fly buzzing around the tofu burger I almost ate! YUCK ☹!

I could NOT believe my friends would actually stab me in the back like this. Even my so-called BFF, Jessica.

I have never been so utterly HUMILIATED in my ENTIRE LIFE!! My reputation at this school is RUINED!!

I'm so upset right now I could just . . .

# SCREEEEEEEEAM!! 😠!

So, Nikki, would you like to know why I HATE you so much?!

NO, you DON'T want to know?! Well, Miss Smarty-Pants, I'm going to tell you ANYWAY!! So just deal with it! Here's my list! The SHORT one!!

# 10 REASONS WHY I HATE YOU!!

1. You CHEATED to WIN the avant-garde art competition!!

2. You totally RUINED my birthday party by SABOTAGING the chocolate fountain!!

3. You competed in the TALENT SHOW and landed a RECORD DEAL even though your application was INCOMPLETE (like, WHO names their band Actually, I'm Not Really Sure Yet?)!!

4. You WON the "Holiday on Ice" show, and EVERYBODY knows that you CAN'T ice-skate!

5. You TOILET-PAPERED my house!!!!

6. You tricked me into DIGGING through a DUMPSTER filled with GARBAGE in my designer dress at the Sweetheart Dance!

7. You actually KISSED my FBF (future boyfriend), BRANDON!!

8. You pretended to be seriously HURT during dodgeball so that I would get DETENTION (which, BTW, could totally RUIN my chances of getting into an Ivy League university)!

9. You put a nasty STINK BUG in my hair!!

And the HORRIBLE THING that I just found out TODAY . . .

10. You've completely RUINED my reputation and HUMILIATED me, because now the ENTIRE school is passing around that AWFUL video of me having a meltdown about the bug that YOU put in my hair.

I am so NOT making this stuff up!!

It's quite obvious you're trying to completely DESTROY my life!!

Things are SO bad at this school that ONE of us has to GO!

It's either YOU . . .

Or . . . ME!!

And if Principal Winston won't KICK you out
of this school for RUINING MY LIFE . . .

# I'M TRANSFERRING TO ANOTHER SCHOOL!!

And I mean it!! I've had it up to HERE with you,
Nikki Maxwell. You are NOT going to get away
with this.

# Just admit it!

If YOU were ME, you'd HATE yourself TOO ☹!

# TOODLES!!

Dear Nikki,

I'm so upset right now I could just . . .

# SCREEEEEEEEEAM!! ☹!

The ENTIRE school has seen that video! And now everyone is laughing at me behind my back.

The CCP girls are giggling.

The CCP guys are chuckling.

The cheerleaders are snickering.

The football team is snorting.

The cooks in the cafeteria are cackling.

I hate to admit it, Nikki! But right now I'm an even bigger JOKE at this school than YOU are!

I was really shocked to see you and your BFFs in school today. I thought you guys were supposed to be in New York City, hanging out with your favorite authors in celebration of National Library Week!

According to the latest gossip, at the very last minute you and your BFFs decided to give your trip to Marcy, Violet, and Jenny so you guys could stay in town and work on the big book drive for the school library.

Sorry! But I don't believe that LAME excuse for one minute!

The TRUTH is, instead of enjoying the exciting sights and sounds of the most FAB city on this earth, YOU chose to stay at school moping around hopelessly depressed, digging through trash cans, scouring bathroom stalls, and searching every nook and cranny in a desperate attempt to find that precious little DIARY of yours!

OMG! I felt SO sorry for you I ALMOST shed a tear. Until I remembered my mascara might run, and goopy black tears streaming down my normally flawless face wouldn't look very CUTE.

Unfortunately, Nikki, you're NOT going to find your diary anytime soon. WHY? Because I'm sitting right next to you in class WRITING in it!

Like, how IRONIC is that ☺?!

And since you're partially responsible for me having such a ROTTEN and MISERABLE day, I thought it was only fair that I do something special for YOU so you can feel the same way.

That's why I tapped you on your shoulder and whispered, "Nikki, I just saw a book that looked exactly like your diary in the library! I think it was on a bookshelf. Or near a pile of books!"

YOU AND YOUR BFFS, SEARCHING
FOR YOUR DIARY IN THE LIBRARY!

YOU AND YOUR BFFS, STILL
SEARCHING FOR YOUR DIARY
SIX HOURS LATER ☺!!

And yes, I realize that tricking you into spending countless hours searching in vain for your diary in the library was a cold and heartless prank.

But do I need to remind YOU of all the SHADY things you've done to humiliate ME?!!

For starters, you CHEATED to win the avant-garde art competition. You're definitely an artist—a CON artist ☹!

That sorry display of the tattoos that you drew was hardly what I'D call art.

Everyone knows I should have won first place!

My brilliant entry could have changed the fashion world as we know it.

My cutting-edge concept would have allowed YOU and other fashion-challenged SLOBS to undergo INSTANTANEOUS MAKEOVERS!!

MY FAB-4-EVER
INSTANT FASHION MAKEOVER KITS

148

My fashions are PERFECT for the cute and trendy girl who was viciously PRANKED into digging through a FILTHY Dumpster for a nonexistent piece of designer jewelry during the Sweetheart Dance!

A girl like ME ☹!!!

And if she's smelling like three-week-old Dumpster juice and has a slimy, rotten banana peel stuck to her face, both SHE and her fab fashion can easily be splashed with laundry detergent and sprayed down with a water hose right in her own backyard!

I could have made MILLIONS on this idea and become one of the hottest fashion designers in the world! But I didn't! And it's all YOUR fault, Nikki ☹!!

Anyway, I've noticed that you and Brandon barely speak to each other now that you've become totally obsessed with finding your lost diary.

It must be heart-wrenching to see your wonderful friendship with him just shrivel up and DIE like a slimy snail on a hot sidewalk.

It's no wonder you look so sad and depressed.

Mere words cannot express the intense emotions I'm feeling right now.

Except maybe . . . YAY ME ☺!!

Sorry I'm NOT sorry!

But please don't get too frustrated about not finding your diary. I have lots of great ideas for where you can look for it.

# TOODLES!

MacKenzie ♡

# THURSDAY, APRIL 17

Dear Nikki,

# Great news!

I've finally found the PERFECT school!

All I have to do now is convince my parents to let me transfer!!

I can't believe this could actually be my very last week at this CRUDDY school!

# YAY ME ☺!!

North Hampton Hills International Academy is one of the most prestigious private schools in the nation!

And it's only twenty-seven minutes from my house. Or ten minutes, if Daddy lets me fly by private helicopter.

Instead of sweaty, smelly sports like football and basketball, it has VERY classy ones, like sailing, horseback riding, fencing, and polo.

And most of the students travel abroad every year. Please don't be jealous, but I'll probably be spending the summer in PARIS ☺!

# YAY ME ☺!!

And since I'm going to have lots of cool new friends, I can't wait to throw a big birthday bash at the country club and invite them all.

Thank goodness YOU won't be around to SABOTAGE my party like last time!!

I was the first person EVER at school to invite a SEWER MUTANT like you to a party!

And how did you repay my generosity ☹?!!

I can almost forgive you for scarfing down all the hors d'oeuvres like a starving barnyard animal.

I know you love wing-dings because they fill that empty void in your miserable little life.

But the coup de grâce was that stunt you pulled with the chocolate fountain.

I know there was a nasty rumor going around at school that my ex-BFF, Jessica, purposely knocked your plate of fruit into the chocolate fountain and splashed chocolate all over your new party dress just to be MEAN!

But that is so NOT true!

Jessica went so far as to PINKIE SWEAR that she saw YOUR dress get splattered while YOU were secretly dumping TRASH into the fountain to sabotage it so it would malfunction!!

## YOU, AT MY PARTY, PUTTING TRASH IN THE CHOCOLATE FOUNTAIN!!

WHY? Because you were insanely jealous that I looked way cuter in my Dior dress than you did in that recycled DISHRAG you were wearing.

But, Nikki, HOW could you be so CRUEL as to DRENCH me with chocolate at the moment I was taking my picture for the SOCIETY PAGE?!

ME, FREAKING OUT BECAUSE YOU RUINED MY BIRTHDAY PARTY!!

I had so much chocolate on me that I felt like a Godiva truffle with LEGS!

Then everyone started LAUGHING at me and taking PICS with their cell phones!

It was HORRIBLE!! For once I was ALMOST as UNPOPULAR as YOU!

I was so FURIOUS, I wanted to . . .

# SCREEEEEEEAM!!! 😡!!

You were lucky you left my party when you did!! Otherwise, you would've experienced what "death by chocolate" really means 🙁!

Now, can I ask you a personal question about something you wrote in your diary?

WHY on earth would you write your USERNAME and PASSWORD in your DIARY?! Do you realize that some very emotionally disturbed individual could steal your diary, read it, and see this highly confidential information just sitting right there on the page?

And if the person is really CRAY-CRAY, she could break into the Miss Know-It-All advice column that you SECRETLY write for the school newspaper (according to your diary)! She could wreak TOTAL HAVOC on the entire student body! With just a few clicks, the entire world as you know it could be completely destroyed!!

Then YOU'D get blamed for cyberbullying, kicked out of school, and—

WAIT!!! ONE!!! MINUTE!!! NO! This CAN'T BE TRUE!!!!!!!!

YOU'RE the real MISS KNOW-IT-ALL??!!

And THIS is your real PASSWORD???!!!

OMG!! I CAN'T EVEN . . . !!

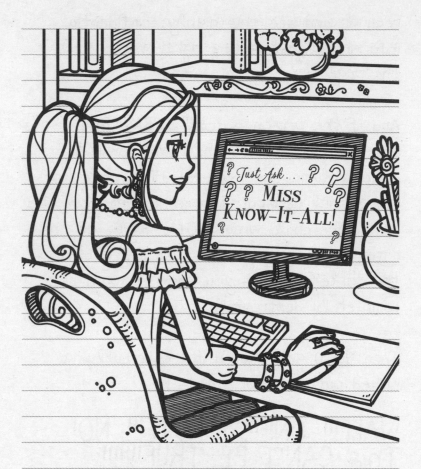

ME, ON MISS KNOW-IT-ALL, SECRETLY VOLUNTEERING TO HELP WITH YOUR ADVICE COLUMN!!

Anyway, you should be thankful I WARNED you that some PSYCHOPATH could steal your

username and password, break into your
Miss Know-It-All website, and WREAK HAVOC
on the entire student body.

You're very LUCKY that I, MACKENZIE HOLLISTER,
stumbled across your information.

And NOT some deranged, vindictive, diary-snatching
DRAMA QUEEN!!

# TOODLES!

Mackenzie

# FRIDAY, APRIL 18

Dear Nikki,

*YAWN!*

I'm really tired today!

Wanna know why, hon?!

Because I stayed up half the night answering letters from the LOSERS who write to your Miss Know-It-All advice column.

I must admit, I was a bit surprised by what I read. I had no idea that the students at this school led such PATHETIC lives!

Anyway, I'm super excited because on Monday, April 28, I have a big SURPRISE for you 😊!!

And when Principal Winston reads the Miss Know-It-All column that I secretly helped you write, he's going to be FURIOUS!!

You're going to get SUSPENDED for CYBERBULLYING so fast it will make your head spin!

Anyway, here are copies of my two favorite letters and the advice I gave:

\* \* \* \* \* \* \* \* \* \* \* \* \* \*

Dear Miss Know-It-All,

I worked really hard to make the eighth-grade cheerleading team this year, but the other cheerleaders treat me like I don't belong. I never get to do much cheering or dancing like they do.

The only time the team captain needs me is when we do the human pyramid, and she always puts me at the bottom! I have to hold the most people on my back, which is totally excruciating, and if I lose my balance, the whole pyramid collapses and everyone bullies me about it!

I'm tired of those girls walking all over me. Literally! I don't know what I did to deserve this kind of treatment, but it's pretty obvious they all hate my guts. ☹!

I'm majorly frustrated! I don't know if I should quit the team, confront my teammates, or just keep quiet so I don't make things worse. I really don't want to give up my dream of making varsity! What would you do??

—*Cheerless Cheerleader*

\* \* \* \* \* \* \* \* \* \* \* \* \* \*

Dear Cheerless Cheerleader,

Hon . . . I think you're kidding yourself if you think you made the cheerleading team based on your awesome moves. My reliable source on the team told me your tryout routine was HOR-REN-DOUS. She said she couldn't tell if you were trying to dance or going into convulsions!

Your backflips were BACKFLOPS, your cartwheels were FLAT TIRES, and your dismount was totally DISGUSTING! Get the picture?

You were chosen for one reason, and one reason alone—you look like a sturdy ogre who can carry a lot of weight! It's been a long tradition for cheerleading captains to hand-pick strong, ugly girls for the bottom of the pyramid. Didn't you know that??

Quit taking everything so personally! Just accept that the bottom is where you belong, sweetie! You should hold your green, Shrek-looking head high that someone actually wants you for something. Bet that doesn't happen often! Yay you!

Sincerely,

*Miss Know-It-All*

P.S. My source wants you to stop dancing. She says you're giving the squad NIGHT TERRORS!

\* \* \* \* \* \* \* \* \* \* \* \* \* \*

OMG! My letter was so MEAN!! OUCH!! ☺!!

Now, this next letter really tugged at my heartstrings. It was hard to be cruel to this poor guy, because he seemed genuinely distraught.

I felt so sorry for him that I actually e-mailed my advice response to him last night.

\* \* \* \* \* \* \* \* \* \* \* \* \* \*

Dear Miss Know-It-All,

I have a good friend, and she's smart, funny, and kind.

But lately we haven't been getting along and it's all MY fault. Between a nasty rumor at school and me not telling her much about my personal life, she doesn't trust me. And I don't blame her one bit.

Whenever I try to talk to her in class, she just seems down and kind of distracted, like something is really bothering her. I'm starting to worry about her, and I really miss our friendship.

What can I do to fix things?

—*Massively Cruddy Friend*

\* \* \* \* \* \* \* \* \* \* \* \* \* \*

Dear Massively Cruddy Friend,

It sounds like you really messed up big-time, bro!

By the way she's acting, it might be too late to rescue this relationship. It looks to me like she wants you about as much as she wants a week-old bowl of moldy oatmeal.

You need to let her know that you care about her ASAP! But NOT with a quick and impersonal e-mail or text.

Since she obviously doesn't feel comfortable talking to you, don't push her. I suggest you write a sincere apology letter and tape it to her locker right before class so that you can see her reaction. Also, make sure you ask her to meet you after school someplace classy so you can talk. Hint: Most girls LOVE the CupCakery!

If she shows up, she truly cares about you and you can consider yourself lucky that you have a very special friendship! Awwww 😊!!!

However, if your friend doesn't show up, it means she's still pretty ticked off at you and possibly never really cared to begin with. If that happens, my advice is to just get over her and move on!

Because, dude, there are plenty of fish in the sea! Including ME 😊!

Sincerely,
*Miss Know-It-All*

* * * * * * * * * * * * * * *

OMG!! Nikki, are YOU thinking what I'M thinking?!

It's very possible that this letter came from YOUR crush, Brandon! YAY YOU ☺!!

And if it did, I'll admit that I'm a little jealous that Brandon wrote to Miss Know-It-All about YOU and not ME!

Unfortunately, he seems to genuinely care about you in spite of the fact that you're a total LOSER!

But sometimes life is NOT fair and people get things that they DON'T deserve!

Most students work really hard to be successful.

And some are naturally gifted, like . . . ME!

Then there are people who CHEAT their way to the top, like . . . YOU!

Yes! I'm STILL traumatized by that talent show!

My dance troupe, Mac's Maniacs, WON because of my mad skillz, edgy styling, and phenomenal choreography!

We KILLED IT!!

Your DORKY band, Actually, I'm Not Really Sure Yet, was a big fat JOKE!

Seriously, Nikki, your singing sounded like a screeching cat with a violent case of diarrhea!

But in spite of the fact that I kicked your butt onstage, it was YOU who became a local celebrity, teen pop princess, and star of your very OWN reality television show!

EXCUSE ME?!! How did THAT happen?!!

You're definitely NOT pretty enough to get by on just your looks like most of the tone-deaf female pop stars today.

But I know your little secret!

You're a MASTER MANIPULATOR!

You BRAINWASH people to make them give you whatever you want!

Or you make them feel so SORRY for you that they're overcome with GUILT and give you whatever you want.

So just enjoy your fifteen minutes of fame while you can, you CHEATING, NO-TALENT POSEUR!

One thing is for sure . . . you will NEVER get invited to attend the GRAMMY AWARDS!

Unless it's to EXTERMINATE the FLIES, FLEAS, and HEAD LICE on those passed-out ROCK STARS who haven't bathed in two years!!

YOU, EXTERMINATING ROCK STARS
AT THE GRAMMYS!

Just thinking about all of this makes me so mad I could just . . .

# SCREEEEEEEAM! 😠!!

But I'm not going to get MAD!!

I'm going to get EVEN! 😊!!

By helping YOU with your Miss Know-It-All column!

And to show you what a great job I'm doing, every day I'll share a few of my favorite SUPER-MEAN letters.

# TOODLES!

MacKenzie

# SATURDAY, APRIL 19

Dear Nikki,

OMG! Yesterday I thought I was going to EXPLODE with excitement! You will NEVER believe what actually happened!

No, I didn't go to the mall and buy you a new wardrobe to replace the tacky clothing you purchased on clearance at Rite-Aim.

Don't LIE to me, Nikki!!

I swear! I saw YOUR JEANS right next to the adult diapers display when I stopped by there to pick up more lip gloss!

Okay, so remember that advice letter I wrote and sent to MASSIVELY CRUDDY FRIEND?

Well, Nikki, guess what I saw taped to your locker right before biology class?! And guess WHO it was from?!

ME, GUSHING OVER THE LETTER
BRANDON LEFT FOR YOU!!

173

Okay, I'll admit that it makes me ~~a little~~ ~~irritated~~ REALLY FURIOUS that Brandon seems to adore you so much.

But can you blame me?!

He's supposed to be MY boyfriend!!

And yes! I was totally DEVASTATED when I saw Brandon kiss you at that charity event!

But then I had an epiphany and totally understood why he did it.

Brandon is a kind, caring, and compassionate person.

Which is probably why he totally IGNORES ME and instead hangs out with all of those pesky, flea-infested little furballs at Fuzzy Friends every day after school!

He's also very cool, super cute, and extremely mature for his age.

Like, how many guys would literally FORCE themselves to kiss a DONKEY FACE like yours in order to save the needy children of the world?!

BRANDON, KISSING YOUR
DONKEY FACE JUST TO SAVE
THE NEEDY CHILDREN OF THE WORLD!!!

Then I ~~started~~ HEARD the nasty rumor that Brandon kissed you on a DARE just to get a Queasy Cheesy pizza!

So, Nikki, I hope you understand that his kiss actually meant nothing at all. Brandon and I were made for each other! He just doesn't know it yet.

And even though you don't deserve it, I DO plan to invite you to OUR wedding when we get married in ten years!

Brandon and I would be VERY honored if you'd agree to be a special guest and participate in our ceremony.

OMG! It's going to be SO romantic when we release a hundred doves as a symbol of our love soaring to new heights in the infinite sky!

And, Nikki, we'll need YOU up front with us on our special day . . .

. . . TO CLEAN UP ALL OF THAT
NASTY BIRD POOP!!

Yes, Nikki! On my wedding day I will FINALLY get even with you for making me scrub those filthy showers in detention! They were the LONGEST three days of my entire LIFE!

SERIOUSLY! That place was an ICKY mildew-and-bug-infested NIGHTMARE! There were more species of INSECTS in there than in the Amazon rain forest!!

I pulled enough HAIR out of the drains to start my own weave business! And I almost puked when I found a hairball the size of a chubby rat!

Sorry to break the news to you, Nikki, but MacKenzie Hollister DOES NOT CLEAN!

Please don't be jealous, but I've had a MAID cleaning up after me since I was three months old.

I thought all I had to do was spray stuff with that foamy cleaner and then all of those smiling Scrubbing Bubbles thingies from the commercial would show up and do all the nasty grunt work!!

But that DIDN'T happen!! I was SO confused!!

So of course I spent, like, two hours CRYING into my MOP BUCKET before my EVIL gym teacher came in and YELLED at me!!

And when I explained that the Scrubbing Bubbles thingies never showed up to help me clean, she said I was "talking crazy" and sent me down to the nurse's office for possible overexposure to toxic fumes!!

Even now, I can STILL smell the faint stench of ammonia, mildew, and "lemony-fresh scent" on my hands. And it's all YOUR fault, Nikki!!

So after seeing that letter Brandon left on your locker, I did what any poor girl would do who was suffering from a very severe case of Post-Detention Stress Syndrome. . . .

Anyway, while we were in class listening to our bio teacher ramble on and on about, um . . . ???

Actually, I don't have the SLIGHTEST idea what that stupid teacher was rambling about. I didn't hear a single word she said because I was totally distracted READING the letter Brandon wrote to you.

OMG! It was so DISGUSTINGLY sweet, sincere, and apologetic, I almost threw up the tofu burger I'd eaten for lunch!

It was very difficult for me to sit in class and watch you and Brandon act like two LOVESICK little LOVEBIRDS!

He stared at you the ENTIRE time, wondering if you'd read his letter.

But, of course, you just totally IGNORED him like he was a huge WAD OF GUM someone had chewed and then stuck under your desk.

ME, READING BRANDON'S LETTER
WHILE HE STARES AT YOU AND
YOU TOTALLY IGNORE HIM!!

OMG! The entire situation made me so ANGRY and FRUSTRATED that I wanted to . . .

# SCREEEEEEEEAM!! 😠!!!

But of course I couldn't, because then I would have gotten ANOTHER detention! And Principal Winston would have forced me to clean those nasty showers AGAIN ☹!!

EXCUSE ME! But I'm STILL suffering from a very severe case of Post-Detention Stress Syndrome from my LAST detention, which was all YOUR fault!

Anyway, Nikki, the good news is that everything worked out just as I had planned!! YAY ME 😊!!

Brandon was so desperate to make up with you that he followed every last detail of my Miss Know-It-All advice letter!

And because you never got the letter he left for you on your locker . . .

HE PATIENTLY WAITED FOR YOU AT
THE CUPCAKERY FOR TWO HOURS,
AND YOU NEVER SHOWED UP!

When Brandon finally gave up and left, he looked absolutely MISERABLE.

I felt SO sorry for the poor guy!

It was quite obvious he was DEVASTATED.

Probably because my Miss Know-It-All advice letter stated that if his friend (YOU!) didn't bother to show up at the CupCakery after getting his letter, it meant . . .

1. She was SO over him! Or . . .

2. She NEVER really cared about him to begin with.

Yes, I know!! You never GOT his letter!

# OOPS!! MY BAD ☺!!

Sorry I'm NOT sorry!

But don't worry, Nikki.

The hurt and anger he's feeling right now won't last forever.

And maybe one day he'll forgive you for ripping out his heart, tossing it in the dirt, and then stomping all over it with your dorky pink high-top sneakers.

# TOODLES!

MacKenzie

# MY MISS KNOW-IT-ALL
# MEANEST LETTER OF THE DAY

Dear Miss Know-It-All,

Could a popular boy ever fall for a nerdy girl?
I have a huge crush on a boy in my chemistry
class, but we hang in different circles. His
friends are jocks and cheerleaders, and my
friends and I are in the chess club.

He's actually really nice and shares some of
my interests. But when his friends are around,
things just get awkward. They bully me and try to
convince him I'm a loser. Although he stands up
for me, I'm just afraid one day he'll believe them!

Yesterday he asked me if I wanted to study
with him at the library, and I almost DIED!
I think he likes me okay as a friend, but it
makes me wonder if he LIKE likes me! I really
want to believe it's true, but my friends are
skeptical. They say popular boys never date
outside their clique.

Are they right, or do you think I have
a chance?

—*Geek Girl*

\* \* \* \* \* \* \* \* \* \* \* \* \* \*

Dear Geek Girl,

Are you kidding me?? Wake up and smell the
caramel macchiato! He's not interested in you,
Boo Boo!

You need to get your head out of your
*Lord of the Rings* book and learn that reality
and fantasy are two different things. Love is not
blind, and popular kids and nerds do NOT mix!
If they got along, we wouldn't need cliques! Can
you imagine how horrible the world would be
without them? Who would I make fun of?!

Anyway, your friends are right to burst your
bubble. Boys think you're gross! As for your
library date with your crush, he's just studying

with you to improve his grades. Lemme speak
in Nerdese so you understand: You're getting
played like a pawn in chess! #Checkmate!

Sorry, but there's no romance in your future. If
you're so smart, why couldn't you figure it out
on your own?! I have better things to do than
waste time on these stupid letters! Now if you'll
excuse me, I'm off to get a manicure.

Toodles!
*Miss Know-It-All*

# SUNDAY, APRIL 20

Dear Nikki,

I am SO excited! Daddy will be returning home from his business trip tomorrow evening.

So I plan to ~~ask~~ BEG my parents to let me transfer to North Hampton Hills International Academy.

I arranged for Nelson to take me to the mall today to buy my new school uniform.

My problem was that I only had $293 left over from my $500 monthly clothing allowance ☹!! And I ALSO needed to buy a handbag, jewelry, and hair accessories to match.

So when Mom gave me $100 to babysit my bratty little sister, Amanda, while she went to the country club to brunch with friends, I decided NOT to have my usual hissy fit.

AMANDA AND ME, TAKING THE LIMO
TO THE MALL TO SHOP FOR
MY NEW SCHOOL UNIFORM!

We arrived at the mall and took the escalator down to the huge, upscale department store that sold school uniforms.

"I love, love, love shopping!!" Amanda squealed. "I'm gonna buy a Princess Sugar Plum purse!"

"No, you don't understand, Amanda! YOU'RE not shopping! I AM!" I corrected her.

"But I wanna shop TOO!" she said, stomping her foot angrily. "Or you'll be SORRY . . . !"

"Excuse me? WHAT are you going to do? Wet your pants?" I asked sarcastically.

That's when Amanda suddenly started breathing really hard, hiccupping, and twitching. Did I mention that my little sister is the QUEEN of kiddie tantrums?

As her shrill voice reverberated through the mall, everyone stopped what they were doing to STARE at us.

OMG! I was SO EMBARRASSED!!

"Amanda!" I hissed. "Shut up before they call security and kick us out of the mall!" But that only made her scream LOUDER!

Lucky for me, I knew exactly how to deal with the little BRAT! I grabbed her hand and rushed past the food court, Toy City, and Puppy Palace to KANDY KINGDOM playland. As soon as Amanda saw it, she stopped screaming and squealed with delight! Thank goodness for short attention spans!

"You can play here while I shop, Amanda. If you need me, I'll be right next door trying on clothes in those fitting rooms with the pink curtains," I said, pointing about twenty-five yards away. "And don't you dare leave playland. I'm going to be keeping an eye on you from my dressing room."

"Okay, bye!" Amanda said, and ran off to join a group of kids on the slide.

Before you judge me for leaving Amanda at playland, put yourself in MY ~~shoes~~ heels.

How could I concentrate on finding the uniform and cute accessories with her screaming her bratty little head off like that?

I could NOT risk a fashion misstep, especially when I have a new school to impress.

Anyway, once inside the store, I discovered a ton of new summer arrivals!

I couldn't resist trying on just a few of them!

Before I knew it, my dressing room was overflowing with clothes.

It was hard to stop because I looked so FAB in EVERYTHING!

"Miss . . . I think you've tried on everything we have in the juniors, designer teens, prom gown, swimsuit, and shoe departments!" the exhausted sales assistant muttered. "Will you be purchasing any of these items today?"

"No thanks! That was just a try-on-a-thon!" I replied. "All I need is the North Hampton Hills school uniform. You can put all this stuff back!"

I don't know what the lady's problem was, but she started doing the same angry twitch thing that Amanda does.

"Of course, miss," she said through gritted teeth. "I'll go get my moving truck and be right back."

Note to self: Get her fired and sue the store!

Suddenly a disembodied head popped into my dressing room.

OMG! It almost SCARED the Mountain's Peak spring water out of me.

IT WAS AMANDA, RUDELY DROPPING
IN TO SHARE HER UNWANTED
FASHION ADVICE!!

"HELP!! It's a big, hairy RAT!" I screamed, and jumped onto a chair. "Oh! It's just you, Amanda. Sorry!"

"Well, I'M sorry YOU look like a PIG in lip gloss wearing a school uniform!" she snickered.

"Why don't you go back to Kandy Kingdom and accidentally fall off the slide?" I said, throwing a sock at her.

"I came to get a tissue for my snotty nose," Amanda sniffed. "I need to get one from your purse, okay?"

"Go right ahead. Just please stop BUGGING me!" I replied. "All this stress is giving me premature wrinkles!" I checked my face in the mirror and gushed. "False alarm. I'm STILL gorgeous!"

Amanda grabbed my purse and turned it upside down, dumping all my stuff onto the floor.

"Seriously?! WHAT are you doing?!!" I yelled.

AMANDA, TRASHING MY PURSE!!

I ignored the brat and went back to admiring my new uniform in the mirror. There was no doubt about it! I was KILLIN' IT!!

Don't HATE me because I'm beautiful!

"Thanks, MacKenzie!" Amanda beamed as she gave me a big hug. "You're the BEST big sister EVER! I LOVE you! Have fun! Bye."

Now, that was a little odd. Amanda seemed REALLY thankful to get that tissue.

I found a leather-and-plaid purse that matched my skirt PERFECTLY! I also snagged the cutest jewelry and hair accessories! The best part was that everything was on sale.

YAY ME ☺!!

The saleslady at the register was super friendly. "My niece and nephew both go to North Hampton Hills. You're going to LOVE it there!" she said after I explained that I was transferring.

She wrapped all my items in tissue, placed them in a huge shopping bag, and then handed it to me.

"Okay, miss! Your total today is $357. Will that be cash or charge?"

"Cash, please," I said as I dug through my purse to retrieve my wallet. But for some reason, I couldn't find it. I giggled nervously at the saleslady and placed my purse on the counter. Then I very carefully looked through it again. Still no wallet.

In a panic, I turned it upside down and dumped it. Everything was there but my wallet. "OMG!" I finally cried. "I can't find my wallet!"

The saleslady gave me a dirty look and snatched the shopping bag from me like I was going to sneak out with it or something.

"I'll just hold on to THIS until you find your, um . . . lost wallet, or whatever," she sniffed.

"Excuse me? Seriously! My DAD could buy me a UNIFORM FACTORY if I wanted one!" I snapped at her.

The cashier glared at me. "Well, I don't know how your dad can buy you a factory if he can't afford to pay $357 for the items you were trying to take out of this store. I have a good mind to call SECURITY!!"

Note to self: Get THIS lady fired along with that other lady. Then sue the store!

"Um, maybe it fell out in my dressing room?" I muttered as I started tossing stuff back into my purse.

When I grabbed a cold, soggy, USED tissue, I cringed. "GROSS!! How did that get in my—"

"OH. NO. SHE. DIDN'T!" I screamed as I rushed out of the store. "AMANDAAAAAA!!!!!"

Amanda was sitting inside the castle tower with a smug grin on her face.

"Amanda!!" I yelled. "Get your butt down here! NOW!"

As she slowly climbed down I noticed that she was carrying a large, blinged-out duffel bag.

"Give me back my wallet!" I screeched.

She zipped open a pocket on her new bag, took out my wallet, and threw it at me.

"If you weren't my sister, I'd have you arrested! And where did you get the money for that thing? You better tell me that you broke into your piggy bank. Again!"

Amanda folded her arms and glared at me.

I opened my wallet and stared at it in shock. All that was left was three dollars!

"OMG! Amanda, I can't believe you STOLE my wallet and SPENT all of my money!! You bratty little . . . THIEF!!"

"I borrowed it! I'll just pay you back on my next birthday when people give me lots of money." She shrugged. "Or I could always get some cash by selling my Barbie doll collection on eBay! Again!"

"Your birthday is ten months from now!" I yelled. "I need to pay for my uniform TODAY!"

"But, MacKenzie, just look at my fabulous purse!" she said, pointing to it. "What do you think? Do you love it, or do you LOOOVE it?!"

"Even though I admire your sophisticated taste in fake Italian handbags, which you obviously inherited from me, you're in SO much trouble right now!" I snarled. "Here's my wallet! You're going to return your bag, get a refund, and put my money BACK inside it. Or I'll tell Daddy what you did and he'll ground you until your tenth birthday! Do you understand me?!"

"YIP!"

I frowned at her. "WHAT?! Was that a yes?"

"No! Um . . . I mean . . . yes!" Amanda stammered.

"YIP! YIP!"

I narrowed my eyes at her.

"Actually, sometimes I make strange sounds when I'm nervous," she explained. "'Yip' means 'yes.' So, yip, I understand!"

"YIP-YIP! YIP!"

I heard it again. Only this time I knew it wasn't her. It actually seemed to be coming from her new purse.

"Um . . . Yip! Yip! Yip!" Amanda barked as her bag started to move.

Suddenly the flap opened and a white furball crawled out and wagged its tail.

AMANDA IS SO BUSTED!!

"OMG! A REAL puppy?" I exclaimed. "Amanda, WHY is there a PUPPY in your bag?!"

"Because all the girls at school are getting a puppy-in-a-purse! So I wanted one too!"

"But, Amanda, we ALREADY have a dog! You can just put Fifi in a purse!"

Of course I made Amanda take that puppy and pet carrier back to Puppy Palace to get a full refund. And boy, was she mad!

We were passing the toy store when Amanda went into another full-blown temper tantrum. I just grabbed her arm and tried to drag her toward the department store so I could pay for my uniform and get the heck out of there.

And yes! It was SOOO embarrassing! But I just totally IGNORED her!

Until she started screaming hysterically.

"STRANGER DANGER! SOMEONE
PLEASE HELP ME!! I'M BEING KIDNAPPED!!"

That's when everyone in the mall turned around and started glaring at me all suspicious-like. I plastered a fake smile on my face and gave Amanda a little hug. "Just calm down, hon!" Then I whispered into her ear, "You spoiled little BRAT!! You better SHUT UP or else!"

"But I want my puppy-in-a-purse! NOOOW!!"

"Sorry! It's NOT happening! I don't have enough to pay for my uniform and a puppy!"

That's when Amanda fell on the floor and started writhing around like a SNAKE. "Get away from me, you KIDNAPPER! HELP! HELP! I'm being KIDNAPPED! Someone call the cops!"

If I got arrested, it could totally RUIN my chances of getting into North Hampton Hills! Lucky for me, I noticed a clearance TOY sale! I quickly offered Amanda a nice bribe if she'd stop screaming long enough for me to pay for my uniform and stuff. She accepted ☺!!

ME, WITH MY NEW SCHOOL
UNIFORM, AND AMANDA, WITH HER
NEW TOY-PUPPY-IN-A-PURSE

In spite of all the drama with Amanda, I'm finally all set for my first day of school at North Hampton Hills International Academy!

I just LOVE my new uniform!

And I'm going to look absolutely FABULOUS!!

YAY ME ☺!!

TOODLES!

MacKenzie

# MY MISS KNOW-IT-ALL
## MEANEST LETTERS OF THE DAY

Today I have TWO letters:

\* \* \* \* \* \* \* \* \* \* \* \* \* \*

Dear Miss Know-It-All,

There is a guy at school who I like. He is an athlete, very cute, cool, and popular. When we are alone he is super nice. But when he is with his friends, he acts like I don't exist. Is he really into me?

Thanks,
*Invisible Girl*

\* \* \* \* \* \* \* \* \* \* \* \* \* \*

Dear Invisible Girl,

If this guy is a CCP, he is obviously out of your league!

He may ignore you when he is with his friends because he is ashamed of you. Guys like him want a smart, beautiful, and rich trophy girlfriend.

I'm sure he is just using you because you are smart and helping him with his homework. Or he's always really hungry and you let him eat the best stuff off your lunch tray every day.

My advice to you is to send me his photo and name because he sounds like my type and we could have a lot in common!

YAY ME!! 😊!!

—Miss Know-It-All

\* \* \* \* \* \* \* \* \* \* \* \* \* \* \*

I'm VERY sure this next letter is from my backstabbing ex-BFF, Jessica.

\* \* \* \* \* \* \* \* \* \* \* \* \* \* \*

Dear Miss Know-It-All,

I have a major BFF problem! Okay, so if I choose popularity over my BFF and toss her out of my life like a piece of moldy, two-week-old pepperoni pizza, does that really make me a bad person? I still secretly adore her, I just don't want to be seen with her in public anymore.

She used to be queen of the CCPs. And when she chose me over all the other girls in school to be her BFF, my coolness factor instantly increased from 6 to 100! I gained lots of cool friends, invites to all the hottest parties, and access to her penthouse-sized SHOE CLOSET!!! I felt like I'd won the BFF lottery!

Then suddenly things changed! Popularity is as fickle as shoe trends—one day it's all about open-toed booties, and a week later they're out of style and everyone is rocking diamond-encrusted ballet flats. Well, the same thing happened with my bestie. She made one little slip-up! And suddenly she's LESS popular than a pair of ugly,

scuffed-up plastic rain boots at a designer shoe
sale. She has lost the special quality that made
me want to become her BFF in the first place.

Now the CCPs are looking for the next It Girl,
and this is finally MY chance to be the girl
everyone envies and wants to be. But hanging
out with my BFF could make ME as unpopular
as she is. I'm even having second thoughts
about inviting her to my upcoming birthday
bash at the country club.

So should I dump my BFF and pursue my dream
of becoming the next CCP Queen Bee (and
just live with the guilt)? Or should I be the loyal
friend who sticks by ~~MacKen~~ my BFF (even
though she's a complete embarrassment) and
give up the opportunity to finally have any
REAL happiness in my life?

—*CCP Princess*

\* \* \* \* \* \* \* \* \* \* \* \* \*

Dear CCP Princess,

Excuse me?! You REALLY should be thankful your AMAZING BFF allowed you to stuff your stinky, SASQUATCH-sized FEET into her designer stilettos!

Seriously, she DIDN'T have to be nice and show PITY to an unpopular WANNABE like YOU! You're lucky she didn't put you on blast when you showed up at Justin's party in that hideous, fluorescent-orange dress your (obviously senile) grandma made for you.

And was that crusty lime-green BOOGER in your nose supposed to be your statement accessory? Or didn't you see that massive, beach-ball-sized thing dangling in the wind when you looked in the mirror? Instead, your very loyal BFF rushed home and returned with a super-cute designer dress for you to wear at the party AND a tissue for that humongous booger.

217

You should be happy your BFF didn't dump you as her BFF when she caught you pretending to be her online just to chat with cute guys! I get it—you want to be her SO BADLY because you can't get a hungry, UGLY dude to look at you even with a FREE bologna sandwich tied around your neck.

Your BFF also could've told everyone your deepest, darkest secrets, like the fact that you wet the bed until you were ELEVEN YEARS OLD! Instead, she upgraded you from a frumpy NOBODY to a CCP socialite, and THIS is how you repay her generosity?! By stabbing her in the back so YOU can become the new CCP queen?!

Sorry! But you'll NEVER, EVER steal her crown as the smartest, prettiest, and fiercest diva of them all! So do yourself a big favor and don't waste your time trying! And don't let me catch you talking mess behind ~~my~~ your BFF's back again!

—*Miss Know-It-All*

Dear Nikki,

I'm sure you've already heard all the gossip about me and my BFF, Jessica. Well, I should say my EX-BFF, Jessica.

Ever since I caught her and my CCP friends making fun of me in that video, I have been so ANGRY that I could just . . .

# SCREEEEEEEEAM! 😠!!

And then Jessica had the NERVE to actually write that letter to Miss Know-It-All TRASHING me like that!

Like, WHO does that kind of thing to another person?!

Well, okay! I'll admit that maybe I do those kinds of things to other people.

But definitely NOT to my BEST friend!!

I was in the girls' bathroom, just minding my own business and putting on a new layer of lip gloss. That's when Jessica came strutting in with some other CCP girls. I could NOT believe she actually had the nerve to ROLL her eyes at me like that.

So I was like, "Jessica! Excuse me, but I really DIDN'T appreciate you making fun of me in that video. But HATERS ARE GONNA HATE!"

And she was like, "MacKenzie, seriously! I have no idea what you are talking about!"

And I was like, "Oh, really! Well, I heard you've been talking trash behind my back just so you can take over my throne as Queen Bee!"

Then it got really, really quiet, and all the CCP girls were just staring at Jessica, waiting to see what lame excuse she was going to give for viciously stabbing me in the back like that.

And Jessica was like, "Mackenzie, I CAN'T EVEN . . . !!"

I could NOT believe she actually said that to me! So I told her off.

ME, TELLING JESSICA OFF
IN THE GIRLS' BATHROOM!!

Right now I'm so OVER Jessica!! I've already unfriended her butt on Facebook. I don't even care if I'm NOT invited to her stupid birthday party!

Anyway, if all of THAT wasn't enough DRAMA for one day, I was forced to watch part two in bio.

It was very obvious that you and Brandon were still upset with each other in class today. He was completely ignoring YOU, just like you were completely ignoring HIM.

That's when I decided to take matters into my own hands.

Maybe if you actually READ Brandon's letter, I wouldn't be forced to sit there and watch the two of you giving each other the cold shoulder.

So after bio today, I took responsibility for my actions and did the right thing!

## I PLACED BRANDON'S LETTER BACK ON YOUR LOCKER ☺!

I was just hanging out at my locker, writing in ~~your~~ MY diary when I saw you stop, stare at his letter in surprise, and then quickly open it.

Hi Nikki,

It's Brandon. Before you ball up this note and toss it away, please read it to the end.

I'm still not sure what happened exactly, but I've been really bummed since we quit hanging out. Biology isn't the same without us goofing off during class and you laughing at my lame jokes. I miss washing dogs at Fuzzy Friends with you, even though we end up getting more dog shampoo on ourselves than on them. And the dogs miss you too!

Was it because of that . . . um, well, what we did at the kissing booth, at the end of the party? And the rumor that came out afterward? I'm sorry if I made you feel bad. I definitely

wish I hadn't done anything to mess
up our friendship.

You said something about how you don't
even know me. So what if we meet
at the CupCakery after school today
and grab some red velvet cupcakes—
my treat! I'll tell you anything you want
to know about me (and not worry that
you'll think I'm weird). I've learned
that honesty and trust are vital in a
true friendship.

If you decide NOT to hang out today,
I totally understand. I guess that
will mean I don't really deserve
your friendship. But it would make
me happy if you would please give me
another chance.

Your Fuzzy Friend,
Brandon

OMG, Nikki! After you read that letter, you were SO happy you went "SQUEEEEEE!!" like a little mouse! Then you started giggling and doing a very weird dance right there in the hall.

You texted the news to Chloe and Zoey, and they ran up, screaming their heads off like you were Taylor Swift or somebody.

Then the three of you did a group hug!

I was a little confused when I overheard you guys planning to meet at your house after school to pick out what you were going to wear.

Then, after you left, I FINALLY realized that you thought you were supposed to meet Brandon after school . . . TODAY!!!

I'll admit the mix-up was partly MY fault!

Seriously, Nikki, I could NOT believe . . .

YOU PATIENTLY WAITED FOR BRANDON
AT THE CUPCAKERY FOR TWO HOURS
AND HE NEVER SHOWED UP!

I don't blame you one bit for being even more FURIOUS with him for standing you up like that! Especially after he wrote you that very sappy letter pouring his heart out to you.

I understand why you feel more CONFUSED than a CHAMELEON in a bag of SKITTLES! Your relationship with Brandon is DOOMED! And it's NEVER, EVER going to work out ☹!

YAY ME ☺!! Sorry I'm NOT sorry!

Anyway, even though you're very disappointed that you and Brandon are SO over, please don't throw a huge pity party for yourself.

Some people have WAY more serious problems than you do! And by "people," I mean girls like ME ☹!!

Right now I'm so MAD at my PARENTS I could just . . .

# SCREEEEEEEEAM!! 😡!

After dinner I tried to have a heart-to-heart talk with my parents about me transferring to North Hampton Hills International Academy!

And as usual they were practically IGNORING every word I said. Daddy was reading the newspaper. And Mommy was checking her hair and applying, like, her ninth layer of lipstick (she's ADDICTED to lipstick).

And in case you were wondering, Amanda was upstairs having a temper tantrum. WHY?! Because when she was potty training her new toy puppy, she accidentally DROPPED it, and clogged the TOILET!

Yes, I know!! That child has SERIOUS issues!!

Anyway, I begged, I screamed, and I cried.

I put on such a theatrical performance that I should receive an Academy Award nomination for Most Dramatic Meltdown in a Family Convo.

ME, HAVING A COMPLETE
EMOTIONAL MELTDOWN WHILE
MY PARENTS CALMLY IGNORE ME!!

I was like, "Mommy! Daddy! You don't understand. The kids at my school HATE me!! Every day I see them watching that video of me with that bug in my hair! And they LAUGH and make fun of me like I'm an UNPOPULAR person or something!"

"Honey, it can't be THAT bad! Just last week you were saying how many friends you have and how much you LOVE your school! The kids just think it's a harmless little joke. I'm sure they don't mean to upset you," my mom said.

"Yes, they DO! Going there every day and dealing with that video is TORTURE! I need to transfer to North Hampton Hills International Academy ASAP! Like tomorrow! PLEEEEASE!"

"Now, MacKenzie, just calm down. It's only a silly little video that kids are passing around on their phones. And by tomorrow they'll probably be watching something else," my dad said sternly.

"But it's RUINING my LIFE!" I sobbed hysterically.

"No, it's NOT ruining your life!" my dad argued. "Now, if this bully, Nicholas, had . . ."

"Dad! HER name is NIKKI!" I screamed.

"Okay . . . NIKKI, then! Now, if this bully, Nikki, had posted the video online, it would be a completely different situation. Then we'd know for sure she had hostile intentions. I wouldn't consider it just a harmless little prank."

"She's obviously upset, Marshall! Maybe we should set up a meeting with Principal Winston," my mom said, looking at her watch. "I have a meeting in twenty minutes about our annual fund-raiser for the children's hospital. So we'll finish this discussion later, MacKenzie, dear. Nelson is already waiting for me in the car," she said as she kissed my forehead. "Toodles!"

"But, MOM!" I groaned. "Please! Don't leave!"

232

"Okay, so here's the plan," my dad said as he turned to the stock market page and frowned at the numbers. "Let's give it another month. If things don't improve by then, we'll schedule a little chat with your principal to get to the bottom of this."

"BUT WHAT AM I SUPPOSED TO DO UNTIL THEN?!" I shrieked at the top of my lungs.

That's when both of my parents looked at each other nervously and said four little words. And NO! Those words weren't "YES, you can transfer!"

They said, "LET'S CALL DR. HADLEY!"

I was like, "EXCUSE ME!! SORRY! But I don't NEED a therapy session right now!!"

If I wanted ADVICE on how to deal with my problems, I'd just write Miss Know-It-All, hack into the website, and send a response to MYSELF!!

"What I NEED is for you to enroll me at North Hampton Hills International Academy! NOW!"

OMG! I was so FURIOUS with my parents.

That's when I totally lost it and screamed . . .

ME, TOTALLY LOSING IT AND
YELLING AT MY PARENTS!!

Then I ran upstairs to my room and slammed the door!

SERIOUSLY! My parents are such IDIOTS!!

They expect me to stay at WCD and ROT while the kids there laugh at me every day like I'm some kind of unpopular LOSER!!

I CAN'T EVEN . . . !!!

HOW CAN MY VERY OWN PARENTS ACTUALLY BELIEVE THIS VIDEO ISN'T A SERIOUS PROBLEM UNTIL SOME HATER POSTS IT ONLINE??!!!

Well, Mommy and Daddy!!!

Guess what?!

THAT can be easily ARRANGED!! . . .

ME, CYBERBULLYING MYSELF BY
POSTING MY OWN VIDEO ONLINE!

Now that my imaginary cyberbully has placed that disgusting video online, my parents will feel SO SORRY for me that they'll FINALLY let me transfer!!

YAY ME !!

North Hampton Hills International Academy, here I COME!!!

TOODLES!

# MY MISS KNOW-IT-ALL
## MEANEST LETTER OF THE DAY

I'm pretty sure this next letter is from Marcy, that shy and very strange little friend of yours. She has BRACES, right?!

\* \* \* \* \* \* \* \* \* \* \* \* \* \*

Dear Miss Know-It-All,

I haven't been my normal, happy self since I was told I needed to get braces.

I'm embarrassed to say this, but when my orthodontist gave me the news, I burst into tears right there in the chair. The truth is, I'm already insecure and this whole braces fiasco is just making me feel a lot worse.

Now whenever I look in the mirror, I imagine an ugly freak with barbed-wire teeth staring back at me. It's a big struggle to get through the school day without crying.

I'm sure you've heard all the horror stories

about kids with braces being relentlessly teased

and called cruel names. Why do people have to

kick a girl when she's already down??

I feel frustrated, depressed, and alone. I haven't told

my friends about any of this because lately they've

been dealing with problems of their own.

But I know you're the perfect person to give me

the encouragement and advice that I need to

get through this! Please help!

—*Blue in Braces*

\* \* \* \* \* \* \* \* \* \* \* \* \* \* \*

Since this girl (Marcy?) sounds like a
complete BASKET CASE, I plan to e-mail
her my advice tomorrow.

WARNING: This letter is so MEAN, it's probably
worth at least a three-day detention!
Sorry, Nikki ☺!

* * * * * * * * * * * * *

Dear Brace Face,

Did I get your name right? Or was it
Zipper Mouth? Maybe it was STUMP GRINDER!
Sorry, sweetie. I'm so forgetful sometimes!
Anyway, having braces isn't all that bad.
Let's look at the pros and cons, shall we?

PROS:
#1: You can get a job at the Olive Garden
restaurant grating cheese with your teeth!

#2: Your mouth also multitasks as a paper
shredder and chain saw!

#3: With all the food you're going to have stuck
in your braces, you'll have yourself a portable,
FREE all-you-can-eat buffet!

CONS:
#1: People will follow you around to get a better
cell phone signal.

#2: A boyfriend with braces could become the kiss of death, literally. If your braces lock up during a smooch, you'll both have to go to the orthodontist together to get it surgically terminated!

#3: On a very clear day, you can pick up interstellar signals from ALIENS on Mars!

Wait a second!! ALL of those sound like CONS, don't they?

Oh well! Too bad for you!

Thank goodness I've ALWAYS had perfectly straight pearly whites!

YAY ME 😊!!

—*Miss Know-It-All*

# TUESDAY, APRIL 22

Dear Nikki,

I thought this moment would never come!

Today is my FINAL DAY at Westchester Country Day Middle School ☺!!

YAY ME ☺!!

Everything worked out just as I had planned.

My parents saw that video of me on the Internet that was posted by that HORRIBLE BULLY at my school.

Namely, YOU!

I was so upset by what you did that I cried myself to sleep last night.

My parents felt SO sorry for me!

So first thing this morning they contacted North Hampton Hills International Academy and arranged for my transfer. YAY ME ☺!!

I totally impressed the headmaster at my admissions interview. She actually said I'd be an asset to their academic institution.

So on Thursday I take the placement tests for all my classes.

As I'm writing this Mommy and Daddy are in the WCD office finalizing paperwork and I'm cleaning out my locker and packing up my personal belongings.

Well, actually, I'm supervising the mover guy.

When I leave, I KNOW you and your BFFs will be standing in the hall rudely STARING at me and wondering what's going on.

But I'll just IGNORE you like I always do! . . .

ME, LEAVING WCD TO ATTEND
NORTH HAMPTON HILLS
INTERNATIONAL ACADEMY ☺!!

And yes! I know there will be a lot of unanswered questions about my sudden departure. But please don't believe any nasty rumors.

The truth is, I'll probably be in Hawaii, on a ninety-foot yacht, wearing a super-cute designer sundress with matching sandals, sipping on a pineapple-mango smoothie, while working on my "Volcanoes in Hawaii" report with the very smart, rich, and posh students in my study group from North Hampton Hills International Academy!!

YAY ME!! ☺!!

Did I mention that most of the students there are the children of celebs, politicians, business tycoons, and royalty?!

I almost forgot to mention that there's been a slight change in plans regarding your diary.

First, I'm totally addicted to writing in it!

And second, I think your diary entries should be shared with the entire WORLD!

Also, don't forget that my final GIFT will be delivered to you on Monday, April 28.

After you're EXPELLED from WCD for cyberbullying, you're going to need a new school too!

And whatever you do, PLEASE, PLEASE, PLEASE don't transfer to North Hampton Hills International Academy ☺!

TOODLES!

Mackenzie

P.S. I left you a little good-bye note and stuck it on my old locker!

# MY MISS KNOW-IT-ALL
## MEANEST LETTER OF THE DAY

Unfortunately, with the transfer and all, today was way too hectic for me to answer any advice letters.

And since I'm going to be super busy at my new school with all my new friends, you can consider this my official RESIGNATION!

I really enjoyed being Miss Know-It-All! Saving a few hopeless weirdos from themselves was a lot like charity work. But most important, it made ME feel all warm and fuzzy inside!

I honestly think this whole experience has changed my life for the better and made me a nicer, more compassionate person.

# NOT!!
☺!!

# OMG!
# YOU'LL NEVER
# BELIEVE
# WHAT
# HAPPENED
# TO ME
# YESTERDAY!!

253

255

# I FINALLY FOUND MY DIARY!!

## SQUEEEEE !!

I'M SO HAPPY RIGHT NOW, I THINK I'M GOING TO GIVE IT A BIG FAT . . .

 ←KISS!

It's been missing for

# TWO. WHOLE. WEEKS!!!...

And the entire time, I've been an emotional

# WRECK!!..

My BFFs and I looked EVERYWHERE for it!
I had pretty much given up hope of EVER finding
my diary again.

And poor Zoey blamed herself for losing it!
She thought it had somehow fallen out when she'd
gone into my backpack to get some gum.

I told her that even if it had, it was totally
an accident and I wasn't mad at her.

But Zoey STILL felt responsible and insisted
that she was the Worst. Friend. EVER!

She'd been moping around, like, FOREVER, and Chloe and I have been worried about her.

But when I showed Zoey my diary, she was so happy she actually burst into tears of joy!

Now I have my diary AND my BFF Zoey back ☺!

# SQUEEEEE!!

The WEIRDEST part is that my diary looked completely different when I found it.

The SNEAKY DIARY SNATCHER had given it a SUPERcute MAKEOVER with a FAB new LEOPARD print cover!

It looked exactly like an expensive designer blouse that I'd seen at the mall for $220!

The day my diary disappeared, I had my suspicions. I wanted to plaster posters of my PRIME SUSPECT all over the school. . . .

# WANTED!!

MACKENZIE HOLLISTER,
FOR THEFT OF DIARY
(WARNING: Cute but dangerous!)

But, unfortunately, I didn't have any proof she was the
STICKY-FINGERED SCOUNDREL who'd stolen it.

Anyway, I could NOT believe all the stuff MacKenzie wrote in MY diary!

I stayed up past midnight and read every last entry. TWICE! She actually gave me a glimpse into her brain.

In spite of her beauty and popularity, her life is not nearly as perfect as everyone thinks.

She just pretends that it is.

And yes, I know MacKenzie is stressed out from all the drama in her life including (1) the detention, (2) the bug video, (3) losing her BFF, Jessica, (4) her insane jealousy of my friendship with Brandon, and (5) wanting to transfer to a new school.

But STILL!! As my grandmother always says, "Everything happens for a reason. And sometimes that reason is you make BAD choices!"

MacKenzie creates a lot of her own problems and then blames them on others.

However, the most SHOCKING thing I discovered was just how DIABOLICAL she is.

HOW diabolical IS she?!

When life gives her LEMONS, she squeezes the juice in other people's EYES!! I'm just sayin'.

I'd actually feel sorry for her if she wasn't so CRUEL.

Anyway, this thing gets even more UNBELIEVABLE!

MacKenzie found my user ID and password in one of MY earlier diary entries and BROKE into my Miss Know-It-All website ☹!!

I'm so NOT lying!!

Then she wrote a bunch of MEAN and NASTY advice letters to unsuspecting students.

Her plan was to get ME kicked out of school for CYBERBULLYING!!

Like, WHO does that?!!!

Thankfully, my Miss Know-It-All newspaper column doesn't publish until Monday, April 28, so I have plenty of time to fix any damage she's done and delete her letters.

In spite of that, I'm STILL a little worried about her THREAT that she has a SURPRISE for me on Monday, April 28 ☹!

But here's the most SHOCKING news of all!!

MACKENIZE HOLLISTER TRANSFERRED TO A NEW SCHOOL!

And yesterday was her last day at WCD!

YES! I know it's really hard to believe! But it's TRUE!! The entire school is GOSSIPING about it, even the teachers.

That DRAMA QUEEN is actually gone from my life!! FOREVER!! WOO-HOO!! . . .

ME, DOING MY SNOOPY HAPPY DANCE
BECAUSE MACKENZIE IS GONE!!

Since MacKenzie is out of the way, I can
FINALLY try to patch things up with Brandon
without HER interfering ☺!

He's been SUPERbusy lately, doing photography for
both the newspaper and yearbook.

We've basically ignored each other and have barely
spoken since that big blowup at my locker a few
weeks ago.

Then things went from bad to worse after
Brandon wrote that really sweet apology letter
inviting me to hang out with him at the CupCakery.

I waited there for him, like, FOREVER, but he never showed up ☹!

I was mad at HIM because I thought he'd stood me up since HE was still mad at ME. And yes! I know it sounds crazy.

But according to MacKenzie's diary entries, SHE was behind the scenes, MANIPULATING everyone and creating all the DRAMA.

I have to admit, I've really missed Brandon these past few weeks. I need to talk to him tomorrow and apologize for everything that's happened.

Anyway, now that MacKenzie has transferred to a new school, my life at WCD is FINALLY going to be DRAMA FREE and absolutely PERFECT!!

# SQUEEEEEE!!
☺!!

NOTE TO SELF:

Chloe wasn't in school yesterday or today, and she hasn't answered any of my text messages.

Which is very STRANGE!

Hopefully, Zoey has heard from her!

But if NOT . . .

1. Call Chloe tonight to make sure she's okay!!

2. Tell her the FANTASTIC news that I FINALLY found my diary ☺!!

3. Let her know that we don't have to worry about Zoey anymore because she's back to her normal happy self. SQUEEE!!

ALSO:

Don't forget to explain everything to Brandon and apologize!

# AAAAAHHHHH ☹!!!

(That was me screaming!)

I thought things would be a lot better with MacKenzie gone.

But today is turning out to be the WORST day EVER!!

I'd already made up my mind that if Chloe was absent again today, Zoey and I were going to stop by her house after school.

The two of us had been calling, texting, and e-mailing Chloe almost nonstop since Wednesday, but we hadn't heard anything from her.

Not even a PEEP!!

What's up with THAT?!!

First Zoey was acting strange, and now Chloe?! JUST GREAT ☹!!

I was worried that something BAD had happened to Chloe on her way to school on Wednesday.

You know, like maybe she got kidnapped by some teen zombies. And they were holding her hostage because they wanted to make her their teen zombie QUEEN.

YIKES ☹!!

Hey, it could happen!

We FINALLY spotted Chloe coming out of the office after second period, Zoey and I were SUPERhappy and nearly HYSTERICAL.

We ran right up to her and shrieked, "Chloe! Chloe! OMG! WHERE have you been?! We tried to contact you! Didn't you get any of our calls, e-mails, or texts?! Are you okay?! Were you sick? We really missed you! Guess what?! We've been DYING to tell you the big news! WE FOUND THE DIARY!!! SQUEEEEE!!"

But then the strangest thing happened! . . .

SHE JUST ROLLED HER EYES AT US
AND WALKED AWAY!

We stood there in shock, staring at our BFF with our mouths hanging open!

Chloe acted like we weren't even there. I could NOT believe she just totally DISSED us like that.

Zoey and I were hurt and confused! But more than anything, we were frustrated by all the unanswered questions.

Why hadn't Chloe bothered to return our millions of phone calls, texts, and e-mails?

What was she upset about?

Why had she been absent?

Was she mad at US?

And if so, why?

But we never got a chance to ask her anything because she SULKED during gym class and was so GLUM at lunch that she refused to even talk to us.

However, Zoey and I were DETERMINED. We were NOT about to give up on our BFF.

So we made a SECRET PLAN.

Later in the day, when the three of us worked in the library together as shelving assistants, we'd be SUPERnice and kind to Chloe to cheer her up.

Then, once she was in a better mood, we'd get her to open up and talk to us about what was bothering her.

And by the end of the hour we'd do a group hug and be BFFs once again. SQUEEEEEE!!

More very soon . . . !!

☺!!!
...

When I left off, Zoey and I were about to implement our secret plan to resolve the CHLOE CRISIS.

"Are you guys as bored as I am?" I muttered, dusting the clean library tables again just to stay awake.

"Well, we could always erase pencil marks from the dictionaries," Zoey suggested.

"I'm not THAT bored!" I grumped. "Do you have any ideas, Chloe?"

Zoey and I looked at her hopefully. But she stared straight ahead and didn't say a word.

"Chloe, what's up? You've been SUPERquiet all day. Is anything wrong?" Zoey asked.

Chloe bit her lip and shook her head no.

"I have an idea. Since we're bored silly, let's play Chloe's favorite game!" I exclaimed. "Charades!"

"That sounds like fun!" Zoey agreed.

"And it beats erasing pencil marks out of dictionaries any day," I said. "Chloe, you can go first."

Chloe folded her arms and just stood there with an unamused look on her face.

"Hmm . . . ," I said, scratching my head. "No movement and blank stare. You're a . . . ROCK?"

Chloe scowled at me and shook her head.

"Well, how about a TREE?" Zoey guessed.

Chloe rolled her eyes for the tenth time today and stood perfectly still. That's when a creative guess popped into my head.

"I know! You're a very ANGRY STATUE?!" I exclaimed. "Right?!"

WRONG!! Chloe gave me an icy stare that was so cold, I almost got frostbite! OUCH!! . . .

CHLOE, GIVING ME AN ICY STARE
DURING OUR FUN GAME OF CHARADES!

I think my very creative guess must have ticked Chloe off or something, because she clenched her fists and stormed across the room.

"Wait! Where are you going?" I called after her. "Zoey and I haven't had our turns yet!"

Chloe shot me a dirty look and violently slammed the library door behind her. BAM!!!

"What just happened?" I asked, totally confused. "Did I miss something?"

"I think we both did," Zoey answered solemnly. "Chloe is obviously angry and giving us both the silent treatment!"

"But why?!" I asked, flabbergasted. "What did we say or do to make her so upset?"

"I don't have the slightest idea!" Zoey shrugged. "She's usually so sweet and bubbly. Maybe she's just having a bad day."

"It feels more like a bad WEEK!" I said with a sigh.

"Well, let's just back off and give her some space. Hopefully, she'll feel better tomorrow," Zoey said.

"If you say so. But it feels like she's HATING us MORE every minute," I complained.

Zoey shook her head and gave a long, sad sigh.

"We both need to be there for Chloe when she's ready to talk. Just remember . . . 'A friend is someone who knows the SONG in your HEART and can SING it back to you when you FORGET the WORDS!'—Author unknown."

OMG! That was the most kind, thoughtful, and sympathetic thing I'd ever heard.

Zoey is the BEST friend ever!

And when it comes to sorting out complicated emotions, she's like a teen Dr. Phil in sparkle lip gloss and skinny jeans.

We didn't have the slightest idea why Chloe
was upset.

Because, unfortunately, our secret plan to cheer
her up . . . DIDN'T.

Zoey and I left the library feeling more worried
than EVER.

☹!!

The situation with Chloe was emotionally draining.

But it wasn't the ONLY DRAMAFEST I had to deal with on Friday.

The other one began when I discovered the cafeteria was serving what looked like deep-fried hockey pucks smothered in a diarrhea gravy.

And smelled like it too ☹! EWWW!!

So I decided to just have a banana for lunch.

I was obviously very distracted about the Chloe Crisis, because when I went to throw away my banana peel, I had a very unfortunate and slightly traumatic ACCIDENT ☹!

With this GUY!!

Only, it wasn't just ANY guy. . . .

ME, ACCIDENTALLY SMACKING
BRANDON WITH A BANANA PEEL!

I could NOT believe Brandon actually said that.

I NEVER, EVER said he was GARBAGE!!

Now, maybe I TREATED him like garbage ☹!

But I never actually CALLED him that.

# BIG! DIFFERENCE!

After my apology crashed and burned, we just stood there staring at each for what seemed like FOREVER!

"So, Brandon, um . . . how are things going?" I asked awkwardly, and plastered on a smile.

Brandon looked down at the slimy banana peel slowly sliding down the front of his shirt, then looked back at me and raised an eyebrow.

"OMG! SORRY! Let me take care of that for you! Don't move!" I said as I dashed to the nearest lunch table like my hair was on fire.

I snatched a fistful of napkins from a dispenser and rushed back to Brandon.

"I'll have you cleaned up in no time," I said, catching my breath.

I peeled the banana from his shirt and tossed it into a (real) garbage can. Then I dabbed at the slimy stain.

"Don't worry about it," Brandon said, looking rather embarrassed. "No big deal. You really don't have to—"

"Yes, I DO!" I interrupted. "Firstly, it was my fault. And secondly, I'm your FRIEND! Although, with everything that's happened lately, it probably doesn't seem like it," I admitted sheepishly.

"Friend? Really, Nikki?! You yelled at me for no apparent reason. Then, after I wrote you an apology letter, you stood me up. Sorry! But with friends like you, who needs enemies?!" he said, obviously a little ticked off at me.

"Actually, I didn't mean to yell at you! That day I spazzed out, MacKenzie was being a major pain, and I seriously thought YOU were HER when I said those things," I explained. "And I DID try to meet you at the CupCakery. But thanks to MacKenzie, I got there THREE days late! That girl is so hopelessly DERANGED, she actually SABOTAGED our relationship with red velvet CUPCAKES! Like, WHO does that?!" I ranted.

"So you're saying all of this is MacKenzie's fault? And she was trying to undermine our friendship again?" Brandon asked skeptically.

"Yes! That's exactly what I'm saying! It's at least partially her fault. Brandon, she's CRIMINALLY INSANE! She started that nasty pizza rumor about you! And I won't even tell you what she's done to me lately, because you'd never believe it. She needs to be locked up in a high-security UNDERGROUND PRISON. In CHAINS!" I fumed.

"Thank goodness she transferred to another school!"

"I'm sorry, Nikki . . . but after all this . . . DRAMA, I don't know what to believe anymore," Brandon said grimly. "Maybe I don't know YOU as well as I thought."

Well, THAT little comment sounded vaguely familiar.

I'd said the exact same thing to HIM during our last argument. I could NOT believe that dude was stealing MY lines!

Suddenly I noticed that the room seemed unusually quiet.

That's when I turned to see the ENTIRE cafeteria GAWKING at us. Like we were a scene from one of those overdramatic teen romance blockbuster movies.

OMG! I was SO embarrassed. . . .

ME, IN SHOCK TO DISCOVER THE ENTIRE
CAFETERIA GAWKING AT US!

As the bell rang signaling lunch was over, Brandon sighed and silently stared at me. He looked like he was deeply pondering everything I'd just said. Or trying to figure out who was more CUCKOO, me or MacKenzie!

"Nikki, honestly, I think we should just . . ." He hesitated and glanced at his watch.

I held my breath and prayed he would give our friendship another chance.

". . . I think we should just get to BIO before we're late. Are you coming?" he asked as he dumped his lunch tray.

That's when I totally PANICKED!

Did this mean our relationship was OVER?

Obviously, we WEREN'T girlfriend and boyfriend. And for the past few weeks we HADN'T even been very good FRIENDS.

So what exactly WAS our relationship?!

And why did it feel so overwhelming? And confusing? And exhilarating? And special? All at the same time.

Then it finally hit me! Maybe Brandon wanted to talk about things on our way to bio!

You know, privately. Without the entire cafeteria eavesdropping on our conversation.

How ROMANTIC would that be ☺?!!

I turned again to look at all the faces STILL staring at us.

Suddenly, I felt a TINY ray of hope! Maybe we could get our friendship back on track after all!

That's when I smiled and finally answered his question. "Um . . . OKAY! Let's get to class."

But when I turned around . . .

BRANDON WAS GONE!

@!!

I came to school early to do a complete review of my Miss Know-It-All letters and search for possible clues about that "surprise" MacKenzie had mentioned.

She had answered about a dozen letters and saved them to my "New Letters" file.

All letters are stored there until I e-mail my advice to students and/or place a copy in the "Auto-Publish" file, which automatically publishes my letters in the school newspaper every Monday at 12:30 p.m.

OMG! Her letters were SO cruel, I cringed just reading them.

And the bad news is that she'd ALREADY e-mailed her advice letters to three students ☹!

After reading about their problems, MacKenzie had guessed that "Massively Cruddy Friend" was

Brandon, "CCP Princess" was Jessica, and "Blue in Braces" was my friend Marcy.

The letter she sent Brandon had created a cupcake nightmare, but he'd managed to survive.

And that backstabbing WANNABE, Jessica, totally deserved the nasty letter her ex-BFF, MacKenzie, had sent her!

But I was a little worried about Marcy.

I made a mental note to talk to her and make sure she hadn't been traumatized by that awful letter she'd received from Miss Know-It-All.

I didn't have a choice but to explain it as a very bad joke and apologize for sending it to her.

I printed copies of MacKenzie's letters (just in case I ever needed them!) and then completely DELETED them from my "New Letters" file.

PROBLEM SOLVED ☺!

MacKenzie's Reign of Terror as the FAKE Miss Know-It-All was officially OVER!!

It was a big fat coincidence that Marcy just happened to walk into the newspaper office as I was finishing up.

And get this! She didn't seem upset at all!

As a matter of fact, she thanked me (again!) for the trip to New York City for National Library Week and gushed nonstop about what a BLAST it had been for Violet, Jenny, and her.

But here's the WEIRD part! When I tried to apologize for the advice letter from Miss Know-It-All about her braces, Marcy claimed she didn't have the slightest idea what I was talking about. She said she HADN'T written a letter to my advice column! Recently, anyway.

Marcy went on to say that her braces weren't so bad once she got used to them, AND she was happy and excited because they were FINALLY coming off in just THREE months!

Okay! THAT convo was really AWKWARD ☹!!

So, MacKenzie was wrong! It appeared that the "Blue in Braces" letter had been written by one of the other dozens of students with braces at our school. JUST GREAT ☹!!

I gathered my stuff and rushed off to meet Zoey at Chloe's locker with my fingers crossed that things would finally be back to normal.

But no such luck! Chloe slammed her locker and walked right past us without saying a word.

It was officially Day Four of the Chloe Crisis!

By lunchtime Zoey and I had come up with the brilliant idea to leave a note on Chloe's locker asking her to meet us in the janitor's closet during lunch to talk.

The three of us always met there when we wanted to discuss important stuff in private.

Zoey quickly scribbled a note from us. . . .

Dear Chloe,

What's wrong?! Are you mad at us? We've been super worried about you these past few days. Do you want to talk about it?

PLEASE, PLEASE, PLEASE meet us in the janitor's closet ASAP! We don't mean to bug you or anything. We just care about you because you're our BFF!!

ZOEY and NIKKI

P.S. We're really sad and miss you ☹!!

Then we folded our letter and taped it to Chloe's locker.

As the bell rang for lunch Zoey and I exchanged nervous glances and rushed off to set up camp in the janitor's closet.

We waited and waited, but it looked like Chloe was going to be a no-show.

That had NEVER, EVER happened before.

Almost overnight it seemed our BFF had turned into a BIGGER drama queen than MacKenzie.

Just as we were about to give up hope, the door clicked and slowly opened.

We were relieved to see Chloe standing there.

She looked really sad, and her eyes were red like she had been crying or something.

"Guys, I've got really bad news!" she said, sniffing.

Those were the first words she'd actually spoken to us in what seemed like a year!!

Zoey and I just stared at her silently.

I got a big lump in my throat, and my heart pounded so loudly I could hear it in my ears.

I was afraid Chloe was going to say her family was moving away to Timbuktu or somewhere!

OMG!

What would Zoey and I do without our BFF?!

I didn't even want to think about it ☹!

Chloe just stood there, kind of trembling like she was going to burst into tears.

Finally, she took a deep breath, pointed at her lips, and then slowly stretched them into what looked like a pink gloss-covered grimace.

"So, you refused to speak to us for all this time because you've been hating on your lip gloss color?!" I exclaimed in disbelief. "Really?!"

Zoey gave me a swift jab with her elbow and shot me a dirty look.

"OUCH!" I whimpered under my breath.

"Actually, we love that color on you, Chloe!" Zoey reassured her as she plastered a fake grin on her face. "It's SUPERcute! Right, Nikki?"

"Yeah, Zoey, REALLY cute! It's actually the same pinkish-red color as the BRUISE you just gave me. You know, before it swells and turns black, blue, and purple," I muttered.

Zoey shot me another dirty look.

"WHAT?!!" I shrugged at her.

Chloe gave us a massive eye roll.

Then she very dramatically showed us her clenched teeth.

Zoey and I could NOT believe our eyes. . . .

ZOEY AND ME, STARING AT CHLOE'S TEETH!

As we both leaned in for a closer look, Chloe smiled shyly (for the first time in days!) and blurted out . . .

"I JUST GOT BRACES!!"

I was so shocked and surprised, I had to restrain myself from TOTALLY freaking out! Chloe was ALREADY traumatized, and I didn't want to make her feel even WORSE.

As she stood there nervously smiling at us, it was quite obvious that Chloe looked ~~adorable~~ ADORKABLE in her new braces.

"OMG! You look SOOO cute in them," Zoey squealed, like she was admiring a new puppy.

"Wow!! Those hot-pink wires really bring out the warmth in your skin tone. And . . . um, the purple brackets complement your eye color!" I gushed, just like those annoying salesgirls at the mall.

Only, I really meant what I said. Kind of.

"Come on! You guys are just saying that to make me feel better!" Chloe sniffed. "Are you sure I don't look like a metal-mouthed . . . FREAK?!"

"Of course NOT!" I yelled.

"Girl, are you KA-RAY-ZEE?!" Zoey screamed.

That's when Zoey and I grabbed our BFF, gave her a big hug, and gushed . . .

CHLOE, YOU'RE BEAUTIFUL!!

ZOEY AND ME, GIVING CHLOE A BIG HUG!

Chloe explained that she was absent from school on Wednesday and Thursday because she was getting her braces. (And to think that I was worried that she had been kidnapped and forced to become a zombie queen!)

"Chloe, why didn't you just TELL us you were getting braces?!" I asked.

"Actually, I did! Kind of," she explained. "But I wanted your HONEST opinion. So I wrote in to your Miss Know-It-All column."

"Are you sure? I never got a letter from you," I answered, slightly confused.

"Well, actually, I didn't use my own name. I wrote in anonymously that I was freaking out about getting braces and asked you for advice. I signed my letter—"

"BLUE IN BRACES!" I practically screamed. "OMG, Chloe! That letter was from YOU?!"

"Yes! I got YOUR letter Tuesday morning, but I didn't get a chance to read it until after school. To be honest, Nikki, your letter made me feel a lot worse!!" Chloe sniffed. "It sounded like you HATED people with braces. That's why I kind of freaked out and stopped talking. I was afraid that if you found out about my braces, you guys wouldn't want to be my friend anymore."

Zoey scowled at me. I quickly scooted away from her, just in case she tried to elbow me again.

"OMG, Chloe! I am SO sorry!" I apologized as a wave of sadness washed over me. "I feel just AWFUL! You did NOT deserve that horrible letter! It probably won't make you feel any better, but . . . I DIDN'T write it!"

"WHAT?!" Chloe and Zoey gasped. "Then WHO did?!"

Up until now, I had been SUPERworried about Chloe and totally distracted by the problems with my Miss Know-It-All column. So this was actually the PERFECT time to finally tell Chloe and Zoey all the nitty-gritty details about MacKenzie.

Starting with the shocking fact that not only had she STOLEN my diary, but she had actually WRITTEN a dozen entries in it.

"Okay, guys, I've been DYING to tell you this! You'll never believe how I actually found my diary! It's a very long and complicated story."

I took a deep breath and quickly rehashed everything, including how MacKenzie had sabotaged my Miss Know-It-All column by writing nasty letters to students and how she had posted her OWN bug video on the Internet. All to get me expelled for cyberbullying.

Chloe and Zoey shook their heads in disbelief.

"I think we should report MACKENZIE for cyberbullying!" Chloe said angrily.

"Yeah, I agree," Zoey added. "We can't let her get

away with this! You should tell Principal Winston and Mr. Zimmerman ASAP. Otherwise, you could end up looking like the guilty person and get suspended from school."

"Well, if I tell Mr. Zimmerman, I can kiss the newspaper good-bye!" I groaned. "He already threatened to FIRE me if I compromised the security of the Miss Know-It-All website."

"But you DIDN'T compromise its security!" Chloe asserted. "Your diary was STOLEN!"

"And it wasn't your FAULT!" Zoey insisted. "You're the VICTIM here!"

"Maybe. But STILL! They'd NEVER believe me!" I argued. "How can I convince them that MacKenzie is responsible for sabotaging my Miss Know-It-All site when she doesn't even attend this school anymore? I have no proof WHATSOEVER!"

"Sure you do!" Chloe smiled wickedly. "And it's in MacKenzie's OWN handwriting!"

"That's right!" Zoey agreed excitedly. "Your DIARY is all the proof you need!"

"Okay, guys, let me get this straight!" I said, trying not to freak out. "I'm supposed to just hand over my diary, which is filled with my deepest feelings, darkest secrets, and most embarrassing moments?! To Principal Winston and Mr. Zimmerman?! As evidence against MacKenzie?!"

"YES!" Chloe and Zoey answered emphatically.

"It's the ONLY way we can stop her!" Chloe argued.

"And the ONLY way you can protect YOURSELF from being expelled for cyberbullying!" Zoey reasoned.

"ARE YOU BOTH INSANE?!" I screamed at my BFFs. "Sorry, but I can't just turn over my DIARY to school officials. There's way too much personal stuff in there!!"

"Yes, I know it's going to be a bit embarrassing, but it's for the greater GOOD!" Zoey claimed.

"Just do the responsible thing and protect students from the real cyberbully—MacKenzie!" Chloe exclaimed.

"But what if it backfires and I get in TROUBLE for all the things I wrote about in my diary?!"

"Come on, Nikki, how bad can it be?!" Zoey asked.

"Well, I wrote that I thought Mr. Zimmerman was crazy!"

"Yeah, Mr. Zimmerman is pretty wacky!" Zoey snickered. "But I'm sure he can take a little joke."

"And even if he gets mad at you, so what?" Chloe giggled.

"And remember that time Principal Winston was eyeballing us at lunch and we started texting each other? I wrote all of that in my diary too! That Principal Winston would never believe we secretly hung out in the janitor's closet. Which, according to our school handbook, is an

307

unauthorized entry by a student and a three-day detention for each occurrence!"

That's when Chloe and Zoey stopped laughing. Their eyes got big as saucers.

WHAT?!!!!.....

My BFFs suddenly looked kind of worried.

"Actually, there's more," I continued. "I also wrote stuff about you guys. Chloe, you said we didn't look like people who would make prank calls from the library phone! And, Zoey, you said we definitely didn't look like students who would sneak into the boys' locker room! I also mentioned how the three of us snuck out of the cafeteria without any passes. That's at least FOUR school rules we've broken, some of them multiple times! But as long as you guys don't mind Principal Winston reading all of that stuff, then FINE! I'll report MacKenzie and turn in my diary as proof."

"OMG, Nikki! You wrote all the things WE did in your diary TOO?!" Zoey screeched.

"SORRY!" I answered sheepishly.

"ARE YOU KIDDING ME?!" Chloe shrieked. "We're looking at YEARS of detention! Our classmates will be seniors in high school and WE'LL still be in eighth grade, serving DETENTION! Do you have any idea how EMBARRASSING that is going to be?!"

"Yeah, and isn't there a rule that after an excessive number of detentions, they just give up on you and KICK you out of school?!" Zoey groaned.

"Sorry, Nikki, but there's NO WAY you can hand over your diary to Principal Winston!" Chloe ranted.

"Totally BAD idea!" Zoey fumed.

"Now, wait a minute! Let me get this straight," I said, narrowing my eyes at my BFFs. "What about the greater good and being responsible? NOW you're saying I CAN'T turn in my diary just because it has a pile of DIRT on you guys?!!"

"EXACTLY!!" Chloe and Zoey answered, glaring at me.

"I'm really disappointed in you two," I complained. "What do you have to say for yourselves?!"

"We're DOOMED!!" Chloe moaned.

"Our lives are SO over!" Zoey groaned.

At least we were FINALLY in complete agreement:
Seeking help from Principal Winston and Mr. Zimmerman
was NOT an option.

If they read my diary, there was a really good
chance my BFFs and I could end up in as much
trouble as MacKenzie!

# YIKES!! ☹!!

"Listen, guys, maybe we're worrying for no reason,"
I said. "As long as MacKenzie doesn't make a move,
we won't need my diary, right? And by now she's
probably in Paris working on a report on the Eiffel
Tower with her posh new friends from North
Hampton Hills International Academy."

"Yeah, but didn't she say something about you
getting a surprise on Monday, April 28?! Well,

that's TODAY! And after stealing your diary and breaking into your website, she's capable of ANYTHING!" Zoey said.

Chloe tapped her chin, deep in thought. "Now, if I were a crazy, jealous, spoiled, high-strung, rich drama queen like MacKenzie, what would I do to get revenge?! Hmm . . . ?!"

"Well, to be honest, I've been really worried that she somehow sabotaged my advice column before she left," I explained. "But as soon as I found out what she'd done, I immediately changed my password so she couldn't log in to my Miss Know-It-All account anymore. And this morning I deleted ALL of her letters and checked everything AGAIN since my advice column is scheduled to publish in the newspaper today during lunch. My new website has this cool auto-publish feature. I just place my advice letters in a special file and they'll publish on a date in the future. But now that I think about it, I FORGOT to check that file."

Suddenly a little light bulb went off in my brain. That's when I totally panicked, and shrieked . . .

"Maybe THAT'S the surprise!" Zoey exclaimed. "What time does the newspaper publish today?"

We all checked the time.

"At 12:30 p.m.!" I said. "Which is in exactly . . ."

"FIVE MINUTES?!!!!" we screamed in horror.

Chloe, Zoey, and I scrambled for the door like we were on our way to a five-alarm fire.

"I'm going to my locker to get my laptop so we can log on to Miss Know-It-All to search for MacKenzie's letters," I yelled over my shoulder. "Could you guys stop by the newspaper office and grab my red folder out of my mailbox? It has hard copies of her letters. Then I'll meet you in the library."

"Okay. But hurry! PLEASE!" Zoey pleaded. "If MacKenzie's letters publish in the school newspaper and you're accused of cyberbullying and forced to hand over your DIARY to Principal Winston . . ."

"WE'RE DEAD MEAT!!" Chloe muttered.

It was actually a good thing MacKenzie transferred to a new school! Because if she hadn't . . . I swear! SHE'D be dead meat! That's just how ANGRY we were at her right then.

MacKenzie had left a ticking TIME BOMB at our school in the form of her Miss Know-It-All responses.

And now we had to find the bomb and defuse it before it EXPLODED!!

!!

When I left off, my BFFs and I were totally
SPAZZING OUT over MacKenzie's letters.

That girl has done a lot of HORRIBLE things,
but THIS stunt was the WORST!

Not only were her prank letters going to HURT
a lot of innocent students, but there was a chance
WE could end up EXPELLED from school! ☹!!

By the time we met back at the library, we had less
than three minutes to find all MacKenzie's letters
and remove them before the newspaper published at
12:30 p.m.

As Chloe and Zoey read over the printed copy
of each letter and gave me details, I searched
for it in my April 28 auto-publish file and quickly
deleted it.

We were so stressed out, we were sweating bullets.
I was typing as fast as my little fingers would go. . . .

ME AND MY BFFS, TRYING TO FIND AND
DELETE MACKENZIE'S LETTERS BEFORE
THEY PUBLISH IN THE NEWSPAPER!!

The good news was that we'd finally made it down to the last TWO letters ☺!! But the bad news was that we had less than thirty seconds to find and delete them ☹!! The situation was HOPELESS!

That's when Chloe said, "Remember, Nikki! If you fail, Brandon and this entire school could be reading your diary next week! So stay focused!"

"Thank you for reminding me, Chloe! But now I feel like throwing up!!" I muttered.

Zoey did a countdown like she was mission control for a NASA rocket launch. "Ten. Nine. Eight. Seven. Six. Five. Four. Three. Two. One! And we have publication of Miss Know-It-All!"

Then my BFFs waited anxiously for me to tell them the fate of those last two letters.

I sighed and gave them my saddest puppy-dog eyes, and their faces fell in disappointment.

It was so quiet, you could hear a pin drop.

Then I screamed . . . "WE DID IT!!" and my BFFs went BANANAS!!

YES! Somehow we'd managed to delete all of MacKenzie's letters seconds before the column posted! We were so happy, we did a group hug.

I was SUPERsurprised when I got a text:

"Chloe and Zoey just crashed the newspaper office and ran off with a folder from your mailbox. Is everything okay? BTW, does Chloe have BRACES?"

It was from Brandon ☺! And since he was actually texting me for the first time in WEEKS, it appeared he wasn't mad at me anymore. SQUEEEE ☺!! I was still pretty ticked off at MacKenzie for torturing Chloe like that. So I replied:

"Everything's fine. And yes, Chloe has braces! But before MacKenzie left, she traumatized the poor girl by cruelly teasing her."

I was SUPERsurprised when minutes later Brandon rushed into the library with a photo. He said it was a little present for Chloe that he hoped would make her feel better. . . .

CHLOE, FREAKING OUT OVER THE
SIXTH-GRADE PHOTO THAT BRANDON
FOUND OF MACKENZIE HOLLISTER

OMG! Apparently, MacKenzie's "perfect pearly whites" hadn't always been SO, um, PERFECT!! . . .

SIXTH-GRADE PHOTO OF
MACKENZIE WITH BRACES?!!

"Why would MacKenzie say all those nasty things about ME wearing braces, when she had them too?!" Chloe exclaimed. "Go figure!"

"Probably because people who go out of their way to make others feel MISERABLE are SUPERinsecure and miserable THEMSELVES!" Zoey explained.

Chloe and I agreed. Soon the bell rang, signaling that lunch was ending and classes would be starting in five minutes.

We couldn't resist gossiping about MacKenzie's braces as we gathered up our stuff.

"Um, Nikki, can we talk for a minute?" Brandon asked, and kind of blushed.

I couldn't believe that Chloe and Zoey were clowning around and making kissy faces behind Brandon's back. They are SO immature!

I was going to DIE of embarrassment if he turned around and caught them doing that!

As soon as Chloe and Zoey left, Brandon pulled up a chair. But I was so nervous that I totally forgot to sit in a chair. Instead, I plopped my behind right on top of the table like an idiot and stared right into his beautiful brown eyes.

Brandon nervously brushed his shaggy bangs out of his eyes and then gave me a big smile.

Of course I blushed and smiled at him. Then he blushed and smiled back at me. All of this blushing and smiling went on, like, FOREVER!!

"Actually, I just wanted to thank you for helping me out with that . . . um, banana peel situation yesterday. And I wanted to apologize for not accepting your . . . um, apology."

"Well, I owe YOU an apology for not accepting YOUR apology too!" I gushed, and batted my eyelashes at him all flirty-like.

"I meant everything I said in my letter, Nikki."

"Really? Well, I'm really glad you wrote it. Even though it got stolen by a crazy drama queen and went missing for three days!" I blushed.

"Anyway, I wanted to talk to you alone because I'm thinking about asking this very special girl to hang out with me. But after everything that has happened, I'm really worried that she might say no. What do you think?"

Okay, that's when I got REALLY ticked off and thought, WHY is this dude even bothering to talk to ME if he is CRUSHING on some OTHER girl?!

Hey, what am I? Chopped liver?!

And then he has the NERVE to ask ME for advice on his LOVE LIFE?! Like, WHO does that?!

I couldn't help wondering if the girl was MacKenzie. Brandon probably thought she was SUPERcool now that she went to that really fancy school.

"Brandon, if she likes you, WHY would she say no?"
I asked quietly.

NOT that I really cared ☹!!

Then he brushed his bangs out of his eyes and shot
me a megawatt smile. But, personally, I didn't see
what was so ding-dang funny.

"So, Nikki, would you like to hang out after school
on Wednesday?" he asked, staring right into the
murky depths of my tortured soul.

OMG! When he asked me that, I was SUPERshocked
and surprised.

And happy! SQUEEE ☺!!!

Of course I said YES! The whole thing was SO
romantic!!

That's when I noticed my BFFs were standing right
outside the door with their faces pressed against the
window, shamelessly SPYING on Brandon and me. . . .

BRANDON, ASKING ME TO HANG OUT
WITH HIM (WHILE CHLOE AND ZOEY
SHAMELESSLY SPY ON US) ☺!!

The good news is that it looks like Brandon and I are finally friends again.

# SQUEEEEEE ☺!!

And thanks to my BFFs, I managed to THWART yet another one of MacKenzie's evil, twisted, diabolical plans!

Even though MacKenzie has been gone for almost a week, she has somehow managed to create more DRAMA in my life than when she was physically present at WCD!

Thank goodness everything worked out just fine with my BFFs, my CRUSH, and my advice column.

Starting today, I plan to start living a happy, stress-free, drama-free, MACKENZIE-FREE life!

☺!!

Losing a diary can be pretty TRAUMATIC!

It almost feels like you've lost a piece of YOURSELF.

Believe me, I know from experience.

I really wanted to tell MacKenzie that I'd found ~~MY~~ HER diary when it accidentally fell out of her moving box that day she left.

I also wanted to encourage her to get a diary of her own and to continue writing in it.

Because sometimes a diary can help you vent frustration, face your fears, find your courage, embrace your dreams, and learn to love yourself.

And it's always better to rip into a page than another human being.

But most important, I wanted to tell MacKenzie

that I FORGIVE her for everything she's done to me in the past few weeks.

Because OMG! She's WAAAAAAAAAAY more MESSED UP than I am ☺!!

I'm just SUPERhappy to have FINALLY gotten my DIARY back!

SQUEEEEEE ☺!!

And I'm lucky to have the BEST FRIENDS ever!

We'll be hanging out after school today to celebrate our friendship.

# SQUEEEEE ☺!!

Sorry, MacKenzie!!

In spite of your beauty, popularity, wealth, and killer wardrobe, I wouldn't want to be you.

Why?

Because, um . . .

# I'm SUCH a DORK!!
# YAY ME!!
# ☺!!

## Operation: Paws!
### Nikki's mission: Hide 7 puppies from 2 parents, an entire school and 1 mean girl out for revenge!

Is Nikki's puppy plan going to end

in a pawfully dorky disaster?!

Find out in PUPPY LOVE . . .

# WEDNESDAY, APRIL 30—4:05 P.M.
## AT MY LOCKER

Okay, I've tried REALLY hard to be polite about all of this! But . . . SORRY!! I JUST CAN'T TAKE IT ANYMORE!!

If I hear MacKenzie Hollister's name one more time, I'm going to . . . SCREAM!!!

I can't believe everyone at this school is STILL talking about her. It's like they're obsessed or something!

"If MacKenzie were here, she'd LOVE this!"

"If MacKenzie were here, she'd HATE that!"

"This school will never be the same without MacKenzie!"

"OMG! I miss MacKenzie SO much!"

MACKENZIE! MACKENZIE! MACKENZIE ☹!!

ME, HAVING A COMPLETE NERVOUS
BREAKDOWN BECAUSE I'M SO SICK OF
EVERYONE TALKING ABOUT MACKENZIE!

Listen up, people! MacKenzie's been GONE for an entire week, and she's NOT coming back!!

So cry yourself a river, build a bridge, and get over it already!!

Okay, I'll admit it.

I was as shocked and surprised as everyone else when she left so abruptly.

But MacKenzie HATED MY GUTS and made my life totally MISERABLE.

And, to be honest, it seems like she's STILL here.

I know this sounds weird, but it's almost like I can FEEL her presence even now as I'm writing in my diary.

But that's probably because the TACKY JUNK kids are leaving for her IS HOGGING UP ALL THE SPACE AT MY LOCKER ☹!!!!

ME, TOTALLY DISGUSTED BY THE JUNK
HOGGING UP MY SPACE ☹!!

I'm sure she's LOVING that her former ex-BFF, Jessica, turned her empty locker into a "We Miss You, MacKenzie!!" shrine, complete with its own Facebook page!

# PUH-LEEZE!!

It's obvious to me that MacKenzie is STILL manipulating students.

Especially after that very pathetic and overdramatic FAREWELL LETTER she e-mailed to our school newspaper this morning.

The editor actually published it online for the entire school to read.

OMG! MacKenzie went on and on about how she was tired of the needless suffering and had decided to end it all by moving on to a much better place.

I'm sure she said all that stuff to make everyone feel SORRY for her.

Just in case I decide to EXPOSE all the TERRIBLE things she did before she left.

Just thinking about all this is making me so ANGRY I could chew . . . ROCKS ☹!!

I know I probably shouldn't say this, because it's kind of rude. MacKenzie reminds me of one of those disposable baby diapers!! Why?

THEY'RE BOTH PLASTIC,
TOTALLY SELF-ABSORBED,
AND FULL OF POOP!!

I STILL haven't gotten over all the mean stuff MacKenzie did. Like stealing my diary, breaking into my Miss Know-It-All website, sending really mean fake advice letters to students, and spreading lies and nasty rumors.

And now SHE'S playing the victim just because of a silly video someone sent around of her freaking out over a bug in her hair?! Yeah, right!

Anyway, MacKenzie ended her so-called suffering at Westchester Country Day Middle School by moving on to a so-called better place. . . .

Namely, North Hampton Hills International Academy!

It's a really posh prep school for the children of celebs, politicians, business tycoons, and royalty. Although, now that I think about it, MacKenzie just might fit in with the royalty at that school.

Because she's the biggest DRAMA QUEEN in the history of the universe ☹!! . . .

MACKENZIE, THE DRAMA QUEEN!

Everyone is also RAVING about her new school.

According to MacKenzie, it has a French chef, a Starbucks, riding stables, a spa, a helicopter landing pad, and a plaza of designer boutiques so kids can shop during lunch and after school hours.

And get this! She said her school has ATM machines in every hall, right next to drinking fountains that dispense seven different fruit-flavored waters.

But MacKenzie is such a pathological LIAR, I was starting to wonder if her FAB school even existed.

I wouldn't have been a bit surprised if she'd completely made it up just to impress everyone, when she's really being homeschooled.

So I googled the school and actually found its official website.

OMG! I could NOT believe my eyes! . . .

Calling North Hampton Hills International Academy "POSH" is an understatement!

That place is AMAZING!!!

It reminds me a lot of Harry Potter's school, Hogwarts.

I just hope MacKenzie is finally happy (assuming she actually even goes there).

Hmm . . . I wonder if North Hampton Hills would award a full scholarship to a very deserving student in exchange for BUG extermination services?

# JUST KIDDING ☺!!

But hey, it wouldn't be the first school to make a deal like that. RIGHT?!

Anyway, now that MacKenzie is gone, MY life is going to be PERFECT ☺!

And DRAMA FREE ☺!

Well, I need to stop ~~ranting~~ writing and get going.

I'm supposed to meet Chloe, Zoey, and Brandon at the CupCakery in twenty minutes, and I STILL need to change into my favorite dress.

The cupcakes there are to DIE for!!

# SQUEEEEEEEE!

☺!!

It was really fun chillaxing with Chloe, Zoey, and Brandon at the CupCakery.

But inside my head I was doing my Snoopy "happy dance" while gleefully counting the number of MINUTES MacKenzie has been OUT of my life! . . .

12,584, 12,585, 12,586, 12,587, 12,588, 12,589 . . . !!

I'M . . . SO . . . HAPPY!!

ME, DOING MY SNOOPY "HAPPY DANCE"!!

The fact that MacKenzie was ACTUALLY gone was FINALLY starting to sink in.

I felt really HOPEFUL and like I had a whole NEW future ahead of me.

I was so distracted that at first I didn't notice Brandon staring at me.

Then he blushed and handed me the most beautiful cupcake with a pink heart on it.

"Nikki, I'm glad we're hanging out again. I know you've been through a lot lately, but I hope everything is okay," he said shyly as he brushed his shaggy bangs out of his eyes.

"Brandon, everything is just PERFECT!!" I gushed.

Then we just stared at each other and blushed.

All this staring, gushing, and blushing went on, like, FOREVER!! . . .

BRANDON AND ME, STARING, GUSHING,
AND BLUSHING AS WE SHARE A CUPCAKE!

# OMG, it was SO romantic!

Suddenly dozens of butterflies started fluttering in my stomach.

It made me feel very giggly and a little queasy. All at the same time. Like I wanted to . . . vomit . . . rainbow-colored . . . CUPCAKE SPRINKLES!

# SQUEEEEEEEEEEE ☺!!

As we stared into each other's eyes, I could definitely sense something KA-RAY-ZEE was about to happen.

AGAIN! Like, um . . . YOU KNOW ☺!!

Chloe and Zoey left from the table near ours to go to the shop next door to get strawberry smoothies. Which meant Brandon and I were alone ☺!

Mere words CANNOT begin to describe what happened next. . . .

355

OMG!! I could NOT believe it was actually . . .

# MACKENZIE HOLLISTER ☹?!!

Somehow she'd just appeared out of thin air.

YEP! Brandon and I were the very unfortunate victims of yet another SNEAKY . . .

# BIG MAC ATTACK ☹!!

MacKenzie had a HUGE smile plastered across her face and was wearing Ready for Revenge Red lip gloss. Which, BTW, clashed with our pink cupcake that had somehow gotten stuck in her hair and was sliding down the side of her face.

She slowly scraped off a big glob of smashed cupcake and licked the frosting off her finger.

"Sorry about that!" she snickered. "My BAD!"

Then she smiled wickedly and said the most ridiculous thing. . . .

MACKENZIE, RETURNING OUR CUPCAKE!

OMG! That cupcake fiasco was so disgusting,
I felt like throwing up AGAIN ☹!

That's when I suddenly realized I was completely
WRONG about MacKenzie. She WASN'T gone from
my life forever!! YET!! But I was about to "fix"
that little problem.

HOW?! By grabbing her wretched little neck and
force-feeding her cupcakes until frosting oozed
out of her ears.

MacKenzie was CRUEL and RUTHLESS! Not only
did she RUIN my cupcake dessert, but she rudely
INTERRUPTED my almost SECOND KISS with
Brandon ☹!

(Which, unlike the first kiss, did NOT involve helping
the needy children of the world!)

I looked right into her beady little eyes and could
see she'd done all that just to undermine my
relationship with Brandon.

"MacKenzie!!!" I gasped in shock. "WHAT are you doing here?!"

"I just came over to say hi. We haven't seen each other in AGES! And wow! You haven't changed a bit, Nikki!"

"That's probably because it's only been a week, one day, eight hours, fifty-four minutes, and thirty-nine seconds. But hey, who's counting?!" I muttered.

Then I totally lost it and screamed, "MacKenzie, next time try staying away LONG enough for me to actually start MISSING you! You know, like maybe twenty-seven YEARS!!" But I just said it inside my head, so no one else heard it but me.

I could not believe what that girl did next!

She totally ignored ME and started FLIRTING shamelessly with BRANDON!!

"So, Brandon, wanna hang out this weekend?
I'll tell you about North Hampton Hills. You'd love
it there. You should transfer!" she said, batting
her eyelashes all flirtylike as she twirled her hair
around and around her finger in a blatant attempt
to hypnotize him to do her evil bidding. . . .

MACKENZIE, SHAMELESSLY
FLIRTING WITH BRANDON!!

"Actually, MacKenzie, Nikki told me everything! Sorry, but I DON'T hang out with SOCIOPATHS!" Brandon said, shooting her a dirty look.

"Well, YOU shouldn't believe everything your little friend tells you, Brandon!" MacKenzie snarled. "Especially when she hasn't been taking her MEDS!"

I could NOT believe that girl was talking TRASH about me right to my face like that. Especially in front of my CRUSH!!

Then MacKenzie scrunched up her nose at me like she smelled something REALLY bad.

"So, Nikki, would you like a Tic Tac breath mint? All that GARBAGE you've been SPEWING about me is making your breath STINK!"

"No, MacKenzie. Actually, YOU need to use that breath mint WAY more than I do! You've been talking so much TRASH and telling so many LIES that YOUR breath stinks worse than my mom's cabbage-and-bologna casserole rotting in a hot garbage bag in July!" I shot back.

That's when MacKenzie got all up in my face like an ortho retainer.

"Nikki, you're a worthless FAKE!! You shouldn't even be attending WCD. Thank goodness I don't go there anymore."

"Oh, really? Well, thank goodness you LEFT! And, MacKenzie, YOU'RE such a FAKE, Barbie is JEALOUS!! But what I don't understand is how you can be so mean and cruel to other people! Is it because you're so insecure? Sorry, but no one is perfect. Not even you, MacKenzie. So you can stop pretending to be."

For a split second she actually looked kind of stunned. I guess I must have hit a nerve or something.

Or maybe she was wondering how I knew she was obsessed with trying to be perfect.

"Unless your name is Google, you need to stop acting like you KNOW everything, Nikki! I'm WARNING you! If you go blabbing my personal business, you're going to regret it. I've read your diary, and I know ALL your little secrets. So DON'T mess with me, or you and your pathetic friends will be kicked out of WCD so fast it will make your head spin!"

"This is between you and me, MacKenzie! Just keep my friends out of it! Dragging innocent people into this is NOT fair!"

"Not FAIR? Really?! You know what THAT sounds like? NOT. MY. PROBLEM!"

I just stared at her in disbelief as she stared back at me with her cold, icy blue eyes. Our conversation was interrupted when several students walked into the cupcake shop.

And get this!! They were dressed in the EXACT same school uniform as MacKenzie!

When she saw them, her mouth dropped open and she looked like she had just seen a ghost or something!

Of course that immediately made me VERY suspicious.

MacKenzie has lied SO often about SO much for SO long, I was beginning to wonder if she really even attended North Hampton Hills.

FINALLY! I was about to find out the TRUTH!
☺!!

## WEDNESDAY—5:10 P.M.
## AT THE CUPCAKERY

<u>OMG!</u> MacKenzie was acting totally SCHIZOID!

Just two minutes ago, she was Miss Thang with a funky attitude, talking trash and all up in my face like <u>NOSE HAIR</u>.

But <u>NOW</u> she was a nervous wreck and more uncomfortable than a fat, slimy worm on a hot sidewalk.

And I was LOVING every minute of it.

She frantically wiped the frosting out of her hair and then said to Brandon and me, "Well, I really should be going now. I have a ton of homework to do. Later!"

But before MacKenzie could sneak away, her classmates spotted her and rushed over to talk.

She quickly plastered on a fake smile. . . .

366

MacKenzie gazed nervously at Brandon and me. "Actually, they were just leaving. They both have a ton of homework to do. So maybe next time, okay?"

But in spite of her objections, her classmates hurried over to introduce themselves.

"Okay! So YOU must be Nikki! I'm Presli. OMG! MacKenzie told us all about her very cool band, Actually, I'm Not Really Sure Yet, and her record deal. It was SO nice of you to agree to stand in for her as lead singer while she had her tonsils removed. Anyway, we want Actually, I'm Not Really Sure Yet to perform at our eighth-grade graduation party, and MacKenzie said she'd think about it and let us know!"

"Hi there! I'm Sol, and YOU'RE Brandon, right?! You and MacKenzie are the CUTEST couple EVER! No wonder the two of you were crowned Sweetheart Prince and Princess at your Valentine's dance. MacKenzie said you'll probably be transferring to North Hampton Hills next year. You're going to LOVE it!"

"Hey, what's up, Nikki! I'm Evan, and I'm the editor of the school newspaper. MacKenzie told us you helped her with her SUPERpopular advice column, Miss Know-It-All. I'm trying to get her to do an advice column for our newspaper too."

"I know the two of you are really missing MacKenzie," Presli continued. "It was SO sweet of you to decorate her old locker! She showed us a photo, and it was ADORABLE!"

"Yeah! How many students would volunteer at Fuzzy Friends, run a book drive for the school library, ice-skate to earn money for charity, AND create a line of designer fashions for homeless animals?" Sol gushed. "MacKenzie's an ANGEL!"

That's when I totally lost it and screamed, "Wow! MacKenzie is just so WONDERFUL! I bet she farts GLITTER too!" But I just said it inside my head, so no one else heard it but me.

I was SO freaked out by all the stuff those kids were saying that I almost fell out of my chair.

It was like MacKenzie had STOLEN my identity or something.

I seriously considered calling the authorities and having her thrown in jail.

# OMG!

Brandon and I were quietly FUMING!!

We were SO mad, our heads were about to EXPLODE!!

But the worst part was that MacKenzie just stood there with this stupid grin on her face, nodding like every word they were saying was TRUE.

## Like, WHO does THAT?!!

It was clear to me why she'd tried to sneak off before they saw her.

It was going to get really complicated really fast with TWO Nikki Maxwells in the room.

I wanted to scream, "Will the REAL Nikki Maxwell PLEASE stand up!"

WHICH NIKKI IS THE REAL ME?!!

Completely fed up, Brandon glanced at the door and cleared his throat.

"Listen, Nikki, it's getting late. I think we should get going. It was really nice meeting all of you."

"Yeah, same here. Hopefully, we'll see you all again soon," I said sweetly as I plastered a big smile across my face, "IF MacKenzie decides to let HER band, Actually, I'm Not Really Sure Yet, play at your graduation party!"

Then I glared at MacKenzie like she was a wad of gum stuck to the bottom of my shoe.

That's when she started to panic.

"Um, wait, guys! Please, don't leave yet. I need to . . . um, explain a few things, okay?"

"Actually, MacKenzie, I've already heard quite enough! North Hampton Hills sounds like a really great school. I'm really, um . . . happy for you," I said.

MacKenzie blinked in surprise. "You are? Really? Thanks! Well, um . . . the least I can do is get you guys another cupcake. You never finished eating the last one."

"Thanks for the offer, MacKenzie. But don't worry about it," I said.

"Are you sure? I hear the double chocolate ones are really good. But my favorite is the red velvet with cream cheese frosting. Or I could buy you BOTH!" MacKenzie rambled.

Brandon and I just shook our heads.

We'd had all we could take of MacKenzie's CRAY-CRAY antics.

All she needed to complete her very bizarre act was some CIRCUS music.

We quickly headed for the door as MacKenzie continued to recite the cupcake menu.

Then, out of nowhere, she suddenly shouted, "Okay, great! It was cool hanging out with you. I miss you, too! Love you guys!"

Okay, THAT was totally weird. What alternate reality was SHE living in?

Or was she just suffering from some obscure disease, like, um . . . early-onset . . . middle-grade . . . DEMENTIA?

Once we were outside, Chloe and Zoey met back up with us in front of the cupcake shop.

"Chloe and Zoey! You'll NEVER in a million years guess who we just saw inside!" I exclaimed.

That's when we heard a strange tapping sound.

The four of us gasped and stared at the huge window of the CupCakery in disbelief.

Finally, Chloe and Zoey uttered . . .

"UM, WAS IT . . . MACKENZIE?!!"

MacKenzie had pressed her face against the window and was frantically waving at us like we were leaving on a cruise ship or something.

Of course we all waved back at her.

Both of my BFFs stared at MacKenzie with perplexed looks on their faces.

"Is she sick or something?" Chloe wondered aloud.

"WHY is she acting so . . . strange? And . . . friendly?" Zoey pondered in awe.

"Listen, guys! Just keep smiling at her and slowly back away. I'll call you later tonight and fill you in," I explained.

Brandon and I said good-bye to Chloe and Zoey and then headed across the street to Fuzzy Friends.

We planned to hang out there for a half hour until my mom picked me up.

Although I hadn't been to Fuzzy Friends in a few weeks, it seemed more like months.

Once on the sidewalk, Brandon glanced warily over his shoulder at the cupcake shop.

"You know something? MacKenzie reminds me a lot of the stomach flu! Just when I think she's gone for good, she comes roaring back with a vengeance!"

"Tell me about it!" I sighed.

It was quite obvious that MacKenzie was up to something. I shuddered at the thought that we were possibly pawns in some scheme of hers.

I couldn't help but wonder whether that illness Brandon had mentioned was CONTAGIOUS.

Because I had a sinking feeling I was about to contract a really UGLY case of the MACKENZIE FLU too!

☹!!

As we walked along, Brandon and I agreed that MacKenzie was always creating DRAMA just to undermine our friendship. Which, BTW, included that nasty rumor that he had kissed me on a bet just to get a free pizza. Of course, I was DYING to ask him about it.

"So, um, did you actually win a FREE . . . pizza?"

"Oh, that?" He rolled his eyes in embarrassment. "Mr. Zimmerman said a camera company donated pizza gift cards to our photography team. So it had nothing whatsoever to do with . . . um, you know." He blushed. "You didn't believe that silly rumor, did you?"

"Of course not! I'm not THAT stupid. I knew all along that MacKenzie was lying! So I didn't believe that rumor for one second," I lied.

As we walked up the sidewalk to Fuzzy Friends, I immediately noticed something strange. . . .

BRANDON AND ME, DISCOVERING
AN ABANDONED DOG!

It was a beautiful, adorable, well-groomed golden retriever.

The dog curiously cocked its head and stared at us. As we approached, it stood up, wagged its tail, and seemed to be really friendly.

"Poor thing," I said. "I wonder who left it out here? And why?"

"I'm not sure. But it doesn't look like one of our dogs."

Brandon stooped over to pat its head and checked for an ID on its collar.

The dog licked his hand and then barked as if to say hello.

That's when we noticed the note attached to its collar.

I opened it and read it aloud. . . .

Dear Fuzzy Friends,

Unfortunately, I had to move into a senior citizen building, and no pets are allowed.

I love Holly very much, so please take good care of her and her critters! I know you will find her a wonderful home.

Thank you for your kindness!

"Critters? What critters?" I asked, confused.

"Hmm. This box says 'For Holly.' So maybe her toys and stuff are inside. Let's take a look," Brandon said.

Curious, we both peered inside the box. . . .

WE WERE VERY SHOCKED AND
SURPRISED BY WHAT WE FOUND!!

Lots of cute, sweet, wiggly little PUPPIES! We had a hard time counting them as they jumped, tumbled, and scampered inside the box.

But there seemed to be SEVEN in all! And, they were TOTALLY ADORABLE!! . . .

"I still have time before my mom gets here. Would you like me to help you take them inside and register them?" I asked.

"Yeah, thanks. But, to be honest, I'd rather we skip all the, um . . . paperwork."

"Then HOW will people know Holly and her puppies are available for adoption?"

"That's exactly my point! Right now I don't want ANYONE to know Fuzzy Friends has eight more homeless animals, okay?"

"But WHY?! I don't understand!"

Brandon closed his eyes and sighed. "This is serious stuff, Nikki. Are you SURE you wanna know? I'm warning you! If I tell you, I might have to KILL you!" he teased half seriously.

"OMG! Brandon, is something wrong?"

"Well, according to our case manager, Fuzzy Friends

has been at full capacity all week. And it gets worse. We won't have room until Sunday morning! He has actually been refusing new animals," Brandon explained as a look of sheer frustration crept onto his face.

"Well, we can just get some extra cages and find some space. How about the storage room?"

"Nikki, it's not that simple. Based on the size of our center, we can only have a certain number of animals on the premises because of the city ordinances."

"Oh! I didn't know that."

"I absolutely HATE when this happens, because we're turning away animals, and not all places in the city have a no-kill policy like we do. So do you know what that means?" He paused and shook his head sadly.

It took a few seconds for me to figure it out. And then my heart sank!

"OH NO!" I groaned. "If Fuzzy Friends doesn't have room, that means Holly and her pups can't stay here! But what if they end up at . . ."

I gasped at the HORROR of it all. I could barely bring myself to say the words.

". . . one of th—those OTHER p—places?!" I stammered. "Brandon, we CAN'T let that happen!! What can we do?!"

"Well, I guess we can keep them here as long as no one knows about it. Including our case manager. It's a serious violation that could get us shut down, so I understand his concern. But I can't put Holly and her pups at risk like that either. I'd NEVER, EVER forgive myself if . . ." His voice cracked and trailed off as he gave Holly a big hug and buried his face in her fur.

She looked at Brandon sadly and whimpered.

Then she licked his face like he was a human lollipop until finally he broke into a big smile. . . .

BRANDON, THE HUMAN LOLLIPOP ☺!!

It was almost like she knew the serious situation she and her pups were in but didn't want Brandon to be upset about it.

Brandon's eyes started to glisten and fill with tears. He blinked and quickly wiped them away.

"Brandon, are you . . . okay?!"

"Um, I just had some dust in my eyes or something. I'm . . . fine," he muttered.

He was obviously LYING! The poor guy looked like his heart had been ripped right out of his chest. I got a huge lump in my throat and felt like crying too.

I felt just horrible for my friend and the eight abandoned dogs he'd already fallen in love with. Suddenly I had a huge surge of energy! Sorry, but I was NOT giving up without a FIGHT! "Listen, Brandon! I've got your back on this! Just tell me what I need to do!"

Brandon cocked his head and stared at me in disbelief. "Nikki, are you SERIOUS?!"

"As SERIOUS as a HEART ATTACK, dude!"

He grinned from ear to ear. "Yeah, me too! I guess I can ALWAYS count on you, Nikki!"

Then we gave each other a high five to seal our deal to keep Holly and her puppies safe until we could find good homes for them.

"So, I hope you're good at keeping secrets," Brandon said with a crooked smile.

Suddenly it became apparent that the task ahead of us was going to be far more difficult than Brandon and I had EVER imagined. . . .

"OMG! DID YOU JUST SAY 'SECRETS'?!" a voice squealed in excitement behind us.

Startled, Brandon and I nearly jumped out of our skins. I could NOT believe someone had been eavesdropping on our very personal and private conversation. We CRINGED and slowly turned around. I was PRAYING that it WASN'T who I thought!!

But, unfortunately, it WAS!! . . .

MACKENZIE! AGAIN ☹?!

It was the second BIG MAC ATTACK that day!

I suddenly got the very creepy feeling that she was STALKING us or something!

"So, what's the BIG SECRET?!! You can trust me. I won't tell a soul, I promise! You guys aren't in any kind of TROUBLE, are you?" she asked, staring at us suspiciously.

Brandon and I exchanged worried looks and then gazed nervously at MacKenzie.

It was quite obvious we were both thinking the EXACT same thing. . . .

# OH, CRUD!!

☹!!!

"MacKenzie, WHAT are YOU doing here?!" I blurted
out for the SECOND time today.

"Listen, Nikki, it wasn't MY fault those IDIOTS
from my school got their facts about us all mixed
up! But that little accident WAS my fault, so
I wanted to personally deliver this," she said,
opening her designer bag and taking out a cupcake
box. I couldn't believe my eyes! Was MacKenzie
actually doing something NICE for a change?

"So the ONLY reason you're here is to deliver
a cupcake?" Brandon asked skeptically.

"Come on! Don't be ridiculous! You think I came here
just to SPY on you? PUH-LEEZE! I have way more
IMPORTANT things I could be doing, like dusting my
FABULOUS shoe collection."

"Okay, let me get this straight. YOU bought US
another cupcake?" I asked, raising an eyebrow.

MacKenzie shook her head and giggled
sarcastically. . . .

"OMG! MacKenzie, you SHOULDN'T have!!" I muttered.

I didn't know which was more DISGUSTING. That nasty-looking cupcake or the fact that I had just thrown up inside my mouth.

"You don't have to thank me!" MacKenzie smiled.

"No, I meant it. You really should NOT have done this! ICK! WHAT is that green gooey stuff?" I asked.

"Who knows!" MacKenzie shrugged. "The waitress at the CupCakery cleared your table and tossed it. But I fished it out of the garbage and brought it here because I wanted you two little LOVEBIRDS to have it!"

EWW! That's when I threw up in my mouth again.

Brandon and I just rolled our eyes. It was quite obvious that MacKenzie had something up her sleeve and was just playing mind games with us.

"What's wrong? You two don't look very happy," she scoffed.

"Why would we be?" I shot back. "You've been practically STALKING us!"

"Well, Miss Smarty-Pants, maybe I wanted to take the scenic route home today!"

I narrowed my eyes at her. "MacKenzie, you WERE spying on us! Just admit it!!"

"Shut up, Nikki! I've got a perfectly good explanation! I was just, um . . ." She hesitated.

I had to admit, MacKenzie looked silly standing there thinking and making weird faces like she was suffering from severe constipation.

I rolled my eyes. "Well, we're WAITING! . . ."

"Actually . . . I was, um. Okay, FINE!" She placed her hands on her hips and glared at us. "So what if I was SNOOPING?! Stop pretending you're so

PERFECT! You dirty, LAW-BREAKING, animal shelter . . . um, RULE VIOLATORS! These mangy mutts, er, I mean . . . POOR DOGS are in extreme . . . DANGER! Thank goodness I got here in time to . . . SAVE THEM!"

Brandon and I froze and gasped. . . .

"So you DID hear us!" I said, trying not to panic.

"Every. Shady. Sneaky. DETAIL! I just hope your little secret doesn't get leaked to the Channel 6 investigative news team," MacKenzie snarled. "Then Fuzzy Friends will lose its license and be shut down! And every last one of these flea-infested MUTTS will be out on the street. Probably getting RUN OVER! Or worse! All because YOU two refused to follow the rules!"

Brandon looked like MacKenzie had just slapped him. He stared down at his feet.

Her harsh words and accusations had obviously knocked the wind (and good intentions) right out of him.

"Brandon, I expected so much BETTER from YOU! I thought you had integrity!" MacKenzie scolded him as he hung his head in shame.

"WHAT is wrong with you, MacKenzie?!" I cried angrily. "You transferred to your dream school and have everything you've ever wanted. Why do

397

you STILL have to DESTROY anything that breathes?"

"Oh, I dunno!" She smirked as she took out her cell phone. "I guess bad habits are hard to break!"

Desperate, I tried to reason with her.

"MacKenzie, can't you see the lives of these innocent animals are at stake?! Not every shelter in this city is safe!" I explained, blinking back tears.

Holly must have sensed I was upset or something because she suddenly bared her teeth, growled, and lunged at MacKenzie.

Brandon grabbed her collar just in time. "Whoa, girl! Calm down! Everything's fine!"

Alarmed, MacKenzie cautiously backed away from Holly. "That dog just tried to ATTACK ME! Keep that thing away from me or I'll call animal control! That savage beast is . . . DANGEROUS!"

OMG! I was SO angry, I wanted to slap that girl into tomorrow. . . .

NO, MACKENZIE! YOU'RE THE SAVAGE BEAST!!

"You say that like it's a BAD thing!" She sneered as she dialed a number on her cell phone.

Then MacKenzie did the unthinkable.

It was like she had stooped to a new LOW and started DIGGING.

"Hello? Is this the Channel 6 news tip hotline? I just found out some dirt on a local animal shelter. I think they're ABUSING animals! Yes, I'll hold."

Brandon looked overwhelmed and totally defeated.

He just sat on the step, staring like a zombie and quietly petting Holly.

Thanks to MacKenzie, Brandon stood to lose TWO things that he CHERISHED . . .

Fuzzy Friends, and Holly and her pups.

His lofty DREAM of helping animals and keeping them safe was quickly turning into his

# WORST NIGHTMARE.

And there wasn't a thing we could do about it!!

☹!!

Calling this FIASCO a nightmare was an understatement ☹!!

MacKenzie was patiently waiting on hold to report Fuzzy Friends in hopes of closing it down.

I had to do SOMETHING! But what?!

I finally came up with four ideas. Unfortunately, each of them had a DOWNSIDE. . . .

1. THE FUNKY PHONE: I could grab MacKenzie's cell phone and quickly toss it into the sewer drain near the curb. Then she wouldn't have a phone to be able to report us.

But I could end up in JAIL for destruction of property. And, even worse, to REPLACE her expensive designer phone, I'd probably have to pay her my weekly allowance for thirteen years, nine months, and two weeks ☹!

2. THE DIVA DASH: Apparently, Holly doesn't like MacKenzie! I could interrupt her phone call AND exercise Holly, by allowing the dog to chase a screaming and hysterical MacKenzie all the way home.

But that would probably be CRUELTY to an ANIMAL! And a little cruel to Holly, too!

3. THE SMUSHED CUPCAKE CAPER: I could take that disgusting cupcake and shove it down MacKenzie's throat. Then she WOULDN'T be able to TALK about Fuzzy Friends (or anything else, for that matter).

But that could be MESSY! And possibly require a trip to the emergency room for doctors to surgically remove both the cupcake and my arm from her throat.

4. THE JUST CLOWNING AROUND: I could convince Brandon to run away with me and the dogs and join the circus. Then we'd spend the rest of our lives performing a funny clown act in SUPERcute costumes. . . .

BRANDON, THE DOGS, AND I
RUN AWAY AND JOIN THE CIRCUS!!

But then we'd miss our family and friends. I've also heard they get VERY SMELLY on hot summer days!

"They" meaning the CIRCUSES, not our family and friends.

After careful consideration, it appeared that the Smushed Cupcake Caper was probably the BEST idea overall.

NOT ☹!!

This situation was HOPELESS!

My mom was going to be picking me up any minute now, and I'd have to say good-bye to Holly and her pups FOREVER!

I sighed sadly and blinked back tears.

I was seriously reconsidering the Cupcake Caper when I came up with a wickedly CUNNING new idea!

Yes, it was a long shot, but it was our only hope!

"Well, Brandon, thanks to MacKenzie, it looks like
Fuzzy Friends is going to be closed down soon,"
I said loud enough for MacKenzie to hear.

MacKenzie, who was STILL on hold, gave me a very
smug look.

OMG! I wanted so badly to WIPE that little
SMIRK right off her face, but instead I continued.

"Anyway, after dealing with all this drama, I've
worked up a really big appetite. So I think I'm
going to head back over to the CupCakery to try
a few of those awesome cupcakes that MacKenzie
recommended."

Of course Brandon looked at me like I was insane.

"Nikki! HOW can you be thinking about CUPCAKES
at a time like this?!" he exclaimed.

"Um, because I'm HUNGRY? Anyway, while I'm there,
I'm going to hang out with MacKenzie's new friends

from North Hampton Hills. They seemed SO friendly. And I'm really looking forward to hearing even more of the fantastic LIES that MacKenzie has told them. But SOMEBODY needs to keep it real and tell them the TRUTH!! Wanna come, Brandon? It should be FUN!"

He finally caught on and gave me a sly grin.

"Sure, Nikki! But let's take the dogs inside first. Now that I think about it, I'd practically KILL for a Sweet Revenge Devil's Food cupcake!"

MacKenzie lowered her phone and nervously EYEBALLED us, all evil-like.

"Don't you DARE talk TRASH about me to my new friends. Better yet, I'M coming with you!!"

"No! You need to STAY right here and save the lives of these POOR dogs!" I said sarcastically.

"Do you think I care about these mangy mutts?!"

MacKenzie angrily ended her phone call and stuffed her cell phone back into her purse.

Then she narrowed her eyes and scowled at Brandon and me. "Listen! You two better stay away from my friends or I'll make sure you never see these little flea-infested furballs again."

"Oh, really?! Is that a THREAT?" I scoffed.

"NO! It's a PROMISE!!" she snarled.

Then she turned and sashayed back across the street to the CupCakery.

I just HATE it when that girl sashays!!

As Brandon and I watched her leave, we sighed in relief.

Thank goodness the dogs were safe!

For the moment, anyway.

Brandon brushed his shaggy bangs out of his eyes and just stared at me for what seemed like FOREVER.

"WHAT?!!" I asked defensively.

Slowly a smile spread across his face until it was ear to ear.

"How did you shut MacKenzie down like that?!" he asked. "I'd pretty much given up hope. I REALLY appreciate what you did just now."

I looked into his big brown eyes and could see he sincerely meant it.

A wave of emotion washed over me, and I got a big lump in my throat. But more than anything, I felt really good that I had Brandon's back and was there for him when he needed me.

Then I shrugged nervously and started babbling like I had totally lost my mind. "Thanks, Brandon!

But YOU'RE a lifesaver! And after we find these dogs a home, you'll be a HERO! You're also a nice person, a good friend, and . . . um, I bet you fart glitter too!"

YES! I actually said THAT to Brandon!!

Somehow it just kind of slipped out of my mouth. I was SO embarrassed.

Brandon and I had a really big laugh at my silly little joke!

"Come on, Nikki! Let's get these dogs inside. I bet they're starving," Brandon said happily as he picked up the box of puppies.

And he was right! Holly gobbled her food and then patiently nursed her hungry puppies.

Then the pups played in their bowl of puppy chow like it was one of those plastic ball pits for toddlers. . . .

BRANDON AND ME, FEEDING
HOLLY AND HER PUPS!

Although we had successfully averted a near disaster, Brandon and I STILL needed to come up with a plan.

We had no idea when the dreaded MACKENZIE FLU was going to STRIKE again!

And, unfortunately, there was no VACCINE!!

MacKenzie is a scheming, conniving SNAKE, so I knew it would be way too risky to keep the dogs at Fuzzy Friends for the rest of the week.

That's when I came up with yet another BRILLIANT idea.

"Listen, Brandon! Why don't we simply take turns taking care of the dogs at our HOMES until Fuzzy Friends has space on Sunday?"

"I don't know, Nikki. Just one dog is a HUGE responsibility. Taking care of eight of them would be EXHAUSTING!"

"Yeah, but it's ONE dog and seven little puppies. And since the mother dog feeds them and stuff, there's not that much we need to do. Come on, Brandon!"

After thinking it over for a few minutes, he finally agreed. "Okay, Nikki! I'll take the first day since they're already here. But we'll need to find more volunteers."

I knew MY mom would definitely say YES to ME keeping the dogs for a day! Just a few weeks ago she'd let my bratty little sister, Brianna, keep

Rover the fish (a classroom pet) at our house for an ENTIRE weekend!

"I'm sure I can keep the dogs for a day too!" I said excitedly. "So now we'll only need TWO more people!"

"Great!" Brandon smiled. "Why don't you talk to Chloe and Zoey, and I'll talk to the guys. I think this plan just might work!"

Anyway, I'm SUPERexcited because I've always wanted a dog! I'd love it and hug it and kiss it and squeeze it and NEVER, EVER let it GO!! SQUEEEEE ☺!!

And NOW I'm going to get the chance to take care of Holly and her seven teeny-weeny, cutie-patootie, snuggly-wuggly, adorable wittle puppies for an ENTIRE twenty-four hours!!!

Hey, how hard can it be?!

Okay, there's GOOD NEWS and some BAD NEWS! First the GOOD NEWS.

When I told Chloe and Zoey about how Brandon and I had found Holly and her puppies abandoned on the front step of Fuzzy Friends, they were SUPERexcited to help out.

So this is our plan: Brandon will be keeping the dogs tonight, I'll have them tomorrow night, Chloe will have them Friday night, and Zoey will have them Saturday night.

Then on Sunday morning we'll return the dogs to Fuzzy Friends so they can be placed in loving homes.

Since Theodore Swagmire's family owns the Queasy Cheesy pizza chain, he volunteered a pizza delivery van and driver to transport the dogs anywhere we need to go.

Okay, now for the BAD NEWS ☹!!

Everything was going as planned until I ran into a BIG, FAT, MESSY, totally unexpected COMPLICATION ☹!

After dinner I was helping my mom put dishes into the dishwasher. It was the perfect time to casually mention the dog situation.

I told her that, due to a family emergency, a good friend of mine needed a pet sitter for his dog, Holly (well, it was kinda true).

Then I ~~asked~~ BEGGED her to PLEASE let me keep the dog overnight on Thursday.

Of course, I conveniently left out the part about the dog having seven rambunctious puppies. I didn't want Mom to FREAK OUT over that very minor little detail!

But after talking to her, it was ME who totally FREAKED OUT. . . .

417

ME AND MOM, HAVING A LITTLE CHAT!

Her LAME excuse about it being "bad timing" made no sense WHATSOEVER!!

What does it matter if the dog has a little accident on the carpet tomorrow or TWO MONTHS from now?!

Either way you just clean it up! DUH!!!

Sorry, Mom, but if you let Brianna keep a pet overnight, then WHY can't I?!!

# It's NOT fair!

Especially since I'm OLDER, more MATURE, and ten times more RESPONSIBLE than Brianna.

Come on! She accidentally murdered poor Rover the fish by giving him a bubble bath, remember?!!

# Like, WHO does that?!!

Mom, if YOU were an ANIMAL, which of these two people would you want to be YOUR pet sitter?! . . .

# PLEASE SELECT
## THE PERFECT PET SITTER!!

☐ BRIANNA,
PET SITTING
ROVER THE FISH

☐ ME,
PET SITTING
HOLLY
THE DOG

I thought so!! I rest my CASE!!

Mom, I don't WANT to keep Holly "maybe in a few months"!

I want to keep her NOW!!

Who knows?! I might be DEAD in a few months!!

And then you'll be at my funeral SOBBING YOUR EYES OUT and rambling hysterically about how you'll NEVER, EVER forgive yourself for NOT letting me keep a pet overnight, especially after you let Brianna do it and she's a lot younger than me.

So thank you, Mom, for completely RUINING my life, endangering eight innocent dogs, and giving me LOW SELF-ESTEEM, which will probably require YEARS of intensive therapy.

Because you obviously LOVE Brianna way more than you love me ☹!!

I need to text Brandon and tell him the very bad news that my mom won't let me keep the dogs.

He's going to be really disappointed. I feel horrible that I let him down like this.

But right now I'm just too upset.

I plan to spend the rest of the night just sitting on my bed in my pajamas, STARING at the wall, SULKING.

☹!!!
...

# AAAAAAAAAAAAAAAAHH!!!!!
(That was me screaming in FRUSTRATION!!)

I have a major project due tomorrow in biology. And it's an entire third of my grade. Things have been so KA-RAY-ZEE the past week that I'd COMPLETELY forgotten about it!

The LAST thing I wanted to do was to procrastinate and then just throw something together the night before, like I did for my *Moby Dick* book report back in December.

I'd made this silly video that starred Brianna as a whale that said "ROAR!!" So I was shocked and surprised when I got an A+ on it ☺!

I decided to finish my SULKING later because I needed to get started on my bio project. Only I didn't have the slightest idea what I was going to do.

Then my mom yelled, "Nikki! Don't forget to take the clothes out of the dryer, fold them up, and put them away BEFORE you go to bed!" . . .

ME, TAKING LAUNDRY OUT OF THE DRYER

The laundry included four pairs of my dad's long underwear that he wears to work on colder days.

They actually look a lot like those one-piece footie pajamas that toddlers wear.

I was about to fold up the last one of them when I suddenly got the most brilliant idea!

Since Dad still had three pairs left, I decided that he probably wouldn't mind if I borrowed one for my bio project.

Besides, he is always harping about how important it is for me to get good grades so I can get a scholarship to a major university. And his long underwear would technically be helping me get a good grade. RIGHT??

So I confiscated them, took out my paint and markers, opened my biology book, and got busy at the kitchen table! . . .

ME, DILIGENTLY WORKING ON
MY ~~DAD'S LONG UNDERWEAR~~
BIO PROJECT!

I finally finished my project a little before midnight,
and I think it came out pretty good.

Especially considering the fact THAT it was based on a wacky idea I had while folding laundry. I just hope my teacher gives me a passing grade on it.

Anyway, now that my bio project is out of the way, I can finish SULKING ☺!!

I can't believe the woman who gave birth to me let Brianna keep a pet overnight but is REFUSING to let ME do the EXACT SAME THING ☹!

# Life is SO unfair!!

I guess I'll tell Brandon the bad news tomorrow.

I just hope we can find another person to take my place.

☹!!

# THURSDAY, MAY 1—2:05 P.M.
## IN THE GIRLS' BATHROOM

I was seriously dreading having to tell Brandon I couldn't keep the dogs.

It didn't help matters that he was happily waiting for me at my locker. Then he went on and on about how great the dogs were doing!

When I finally got up the courage to break the news, I interrupted him and said, "Um, Brandon, there's something really important I need to tell you."

But he said, "Really? Because there's something really important I need to tell YOU!"

He started gushing about how thankful and lucky he was to have me as a friend!!

Which made it even MORE difficult for me to tell him.

Then he said, "So, I'll drop the dogs by your house right after school today, okay?"

428

But before I could answer and say, "Actually, Brandon, you CAN'T drop the dogs by my house!! That's what I've been trying to tell you for the past ten minutes," he said, "Later, Nikki! See you in bio!" and disappeared into the crowded hallway.

The whole thing was SO FRUSTRATING ☹!!!

So now I had to try to explain everything to him AGAIN when I saw him in bio.

Only right before bio, I went into the girls' bathroom and stood in front of the mirror and practiced telling Brandon the bad news.

But I practiced too long and ended up four minutes late for bio, which meant I completely missed the chance to tell him the bad news AGAIN!

I just KNEW my teacher was going to be SUPERirritated with me for handing my project in late, and maybe even take a few points off.

But the strangest thing happened. . . .

My teacher actually LOVED my project!

She said it was not only creative, but very realistic.

As a matter of fact, she was SO impressed that she asked for a volunteer to WEAR it while she taught today's lesson on the human body.

Then she waited patiently for a student to raise his/her hand.

But I already knew she was wasting her time.

Who'd be STUPID enough to wear my dad's long underwear with the HUMAN ANATOMY painted on it in front of a classroom of their middle-school peers?!

Well, okay!

I'll rephrase the question. . . .

WHO, other than ME, would be that STUPID?! . . .

CLASS, THIS IS WHAT COMPLETE
HUMILIATION LOOKS LIKE!!

Most of the students must have thought the lesson was hilarious, because they snickered and giggled the entire time I was up there.

OMG! I was SO embarrassed.

I looked like some . . . FREAK who'd been in a really bad . . . parachuting accident and had somehow gotten . . . turned inside out.

Anyway, after class was over my teacher thanked me for creating such a wonderful project and sharing it with my classmates.

Then she suggested I enter it in the citywide science fair that our school would be hosting tomorrow after school.

Like, WHY would I want to HUMILIATE myself in front of the ENTIRE city?!

That's when I completely lost it and screamed, "I'm really SORRY, Ms. Kincaid! But I can't discuss the science fair right now. I need to rush outside, dig a really deep hole, crawl into it, and DIE!!"

Of course, I just said it inside my head, so no one else heard it but me.

Right now I'm hiding out in the girls' bathroom writing all this.

Unfortunately, I'll probably NEVER be able to do the laundry again. WHY?

Because I'm ALLERGIC to LONG UNDERWEAR!!

Anyway, I never got a chance to talk to Brandon.

So I've decided NOT to tell him!

Instead, I'm going to keep the dogs as planned.

I'll just HIDE them in my bedroom the entire time so that Mom and Dad will never even know they're in the house.

I'm sure the dogs will mostly just hang out in their cage and eat and sleep all day long.

And since the mother dog is there watching her puppies, that means LESS work for me!

Besides, I'll only be HIDING them in my room for twenty-four hours!

Hey, how hard can it be?!

!!

I thought the school day would NEVER end! I was DYING to go home so I could get everything ready for Holly and her puppies.

First I cleaned my room (the last thing I wanted was for one of the dogs to nibble on that ten-day-old moldy pizza slice under my bed). Then I puppy-proofed it (my room, not the pizza).

And just in case Brianna decided to SNOOP around once she got home from school, I cleared out enough space in my closet to hide the dog cage.

When Brandon finally dropped off the dogs, I excitedly took them upstairs to my bedroom.

OMG! They were so CUTE, I almost . . . melted into a . . . puddle of . . . sweet, sticky . . . um, goo!

When Chloe and Zoey came over to visit, they immediately fell in love with the dogs too. . . .

CHLOE AND ZOEY MEET THE DOGS!!

Holly and one sleepy puppy took a little nap, while the six other pups ran around my room, getting into all kinds of mischief.

The smallest puppy cuddled with Brianna's teddy bear, one chewed on a gym sock, while another played hide-and-seek under my bed.

# They were SO cute !!

I told Chloe and Zoey that my only worry was having to leave the dogs alone in my bedroom for extended periods, like during meals.

That's when Chloe said she had already thought about that problem and had come up with the PERFECT solution. She reached into her backpack and took out what looked like two old-fashioned cell phones.

Then she said . . .

CHLOE GIVES ME A BABY MONITOR SET
FOR THE DOGS!

Her mom had used it for Chloe's little brother when he was an infant.

Chloe explained that I was supposed to leave the speaker unit in my bedroom with the dogs and take the receiver part with me.

Then I'd be able to hear what the dogs were up to in my bedroom. Now, how COOL is THAT ☺?!! This baby monitor was a brilliant idea and would make taking care of the dogs A LOT easier.

"Until you decide to use them, I think we need to hide them somewhere," Chloe said, looking around the room. She grabbed my backpack off my chair and placed the baby monitor set inside. "Perfect!"

"Thanks, Chloe! Now, if I could only get rid of my parents for the entire evening! I'm afraid they might hear the dogs!"

That's when Zoey said she had already thought about that problem and had come up with the PERFECT solution.

She reached into her purse. "Here, Nikki! TWO MOVIE TICKETS!!" she exclaimed.

"Thanks, Zoey! But how am I supposed to take eight dogs to a MOVIE?!!" I asked, confused.

"They're NOT for YOU, silly! They're for your PARENTS! I bought tickets for the prequel of that new sci-fi blockbuster! It lasts three and a half hours! With the travel time there and back, your parents will be out of the house AND out of your hair for most of the night!"

I gave Chloe and Zoey a really big HUG! They're the BEST BFFs EVER!!

Thanks to them, I was going to be the PERFECT PET SITTER!!

☺!!

At first I was going to keep the dogs a secret from Brianna.

Mainly because she has a nasty habit of BLABBING any and everything to Mom and Dad.

But there was no way I was going to be able to hide eight dogs from Mom and Dad without a little help.

I didn't have a choice but to trust her.

Do you want to know the ONLY thing more exhausting than taking care of Brianna?

Taking care of SEVEN little Briannas with bigger ears and more hair on their backs.

So it was no surprise when they fell completely head over heels in love with each other at first sight. . . .

BRIANNA HUGS HOLLY AND HER PUPPIES!

I didn't realize how much she and the puppies had in common:

1. They're really loud and smell funny.

2. They're wiggly, messy, and like following me around the house.

3. They could use some additional potty training.

AND

4. They can get away with practically anything because they're SO ridiculously CUTE!!

They're like sisters and brothers from another mother!

However, the downside is that now Brianna is pestering me nonstop about "playing with the doggies."

I was in the kitchen doing my geometry homework when she walked in.

"Nikki! Can I let the doggies out of their cage and play with them for a little while? PLEASE! PLEASE! PLEASE! PLEASE! PLEASE!"

"Not until I finish my homework, Brianna. If you let them out of their cage, you have to keep a close eye on the puppies. Or else they'll get into trouble."

Brianna pondered what I'd just said and tapped her chin in thought. "Trouble? Like, what kind of trouble?" she asked.

"Brianna, if you let the dogs out of their cage, they can get into all SORTS of trouble! Okay?"

"So, do you mean trouble like tearing up the pillows, digging up Mom's plant, and pooping in Dad's favorite chair?" she asked casually, and then batted her eyes all innocentlike.

I turned and stared at my little sister in disbelief.

"Brianna! Don't tell me you let the dogs out of their cage?!" I groaned as I slammed my book shut.

There was just NO WAY I was going to finish my homework while babysitting ~~eight~~ NINE unruly animals.

"Okay! If you DON'T want me to tell you that I let the dogs out of their cage, then I WON'T! Can I have a cookie?" Brianna quipped.

OMG! I was SO mad at Brianna that I wanted to release all my frustration by screaming into a pillow.

But I couldn't, because the puppies were busily pulling every ounce of stuffing out of each one.

Cotton was scattered everywhere.

It looked like there had been a major snowstorm right in the family room.

That's when Brianna pointed and said . . .

"JUST GREAT!!" I sighed. "Okay, Brianna! Here's your chance. You can take care of the dogs while I clean up this mess. If Mom and Dad see this, I'M DEAD MEAT!"

"Thank you, Nikki!" Brianna squealed. "I'm gonna be the best doggie sitter EVER! I got lots of practice taking care of Rover the fish a few weeks ago, remember?"

How could I forget?

"Please! Don't remind me!" I exclaimed. "Just take the dogs up to my room and keep them out of trouble. And don't forget the doggie snacks. You're going to need 'em!" I said, handing her a box of doggie doughnuts.

Brianna tossed one into her mouth and chewed. "YUM!! It's bacon-'n'-cheese! I LOVE these things!"

"They're not for you, silly! If you offer the pups a doggie snack, they'll follow you anywhere."

"Oh! I knew that!" Brianna grinned sheepishly.
"Who wants a doggie snack?!" she asked, waving
one in the air.

The dogs immediately stopped unstuffing the
pillows and happily scampered up the stairs after
Brianna and the doggie snack.

I have to admit, it was really nice to have a little
"me time" away from Brianna and the dogs.

Frantically restuffing and sewing pillows while
pricking my fingers bloody was actually a
lot EASIER than trying to entertain eight
rambunctious dogs and one bratty little sister.

But forty-five minutes later, as I was finishing up,
I was suddenly overcome with paranoia.

At first I thought I was feeling faint due to the
loss of blood.

But I couldn't exactly put my finger on it.

Probably because they were numb from being poked with the needle over and over.

Something was just . . .

# WRONG!

Finally I figured it out.

"It's quiet. TOO quiet!" I muttered to myself. "Brianna is up to something!"

That's when I raced toward the stairs.

"Brianna! What are you doing with the dogs?!" I yelled on my way up. But there was no reply. "You'd better answer me, or else. . . ."

At the top of the stairs I found a sign, sloppily written in red crayon.

It was Brianna's handwriting!! . . .

**QWIET PLEEZ!**

**WELCOME to**

**MISS BRI-BRI'S**

**PAW SPA**

There was yet another sign farther down the hall that said . . .

Of course, I decided to totally ignore her VERY RUDE and unprofessional signs.

452

I had a good mind to report PAW SPA to the Better Business Bureau. But I digress. . . .

I followed the sound of classical spa music toward Brianna's bedroom.

That's when I noticed that Mom's battery-powered candles gently lit the hallway, while the floor had been sprinkled with flower petals for dramatic effect.

"Wow. Brianna really went all out for this make-believe spa," I thought. "The pink rose petals are actually a nice touch!"

But she didn't stop at just the roses. A few feet down the hall she had scattered lilacs and gardenias.

"Wait a minute. . . ." I frowned. "Where did she get these?!" For some reason, they looked awfully familiar.

Okay, I was starting to get nervous.

Near my bedroom door I saw scattered leaves, shrubbery, twigs, and . . . roots?!

Which made me VERY worried.

But I totally lost it when I saw the fresh dirt and confused worms scattered over Mom's new rug!

Brianna's bedroom door was locked, so I pounded on it with my fists.

"BRIANNAAAAAAAAA!!!!" I screamed. "I can't believe you completely MUTILATED Mrs. Wallabanger's prizewinning flower garden!!"

That's when a strange little woman wearing fake-diamond cat-eye glasses, a long scarf, a kiddie paint apron filled with Mom's spa essentials collection, six-sizes-too-big red heels, and way too much makeup and jewelry very cautiously opened Brianna's door and poked her head out.

She glared at me, scrunched up her nose, and hissed . . .

ME, BEING SHUSHED BY A
STRANGE LITTLE WOMAN!

I couldn't believe my eyes! It was . . .

# Miss Bri-Bri ☹?!

Also known as Madame Bri-Bri, Fashionista Hairstylist to the Stars.

And now, apparently, the owner of the trendy new PAW SPA for non-"hoomans"!

She stared at me as I stared at her.

I knew right then and there that I was in for a . . .

## VERY!

## LONG!!

## NIGHT!!!

!!

"SHHHHHH! Zis eez a relaxation spa, dah-ling!" Miss Bri-Bri scolded me. "Did you not understand zee sign?!"

"First of all, don't you dare SHUSH me! I'm the one in charge here!" I shot back. "Second of all, your signs were barely legible! I hate to break it to you, madame, but you can't spell worth BEANS!"

"Sorry, I know nothing about zee beans that you speak of. Miss Bri-Bri eez very busy, dah-ling! Unless you are a puppy with le spa reservation, I must ask you to leave. We enforce a strict 'no hoomans allowed' policy! Read zee sign, please!"

Then she slammed the door right in my face. BAM!!

"Miss Bri-Bri! Er, I mean . . . BRIANNA, I'm about three seconds from going APE CRAZY on you if you don't open this door!" I growled. "ONE!! . . . TWO!! . . . THREE!! . . ."

Suddenly the door was flung open.

"Dah-ling! Please! You MUST calm down. Or I'll be forced to call SECURITY. BUT if you agree to keep all of zee flowers you saw in zee hall a big SECRET, then Miss Bri-Bri will give you a DISCOUNT on le peanut butter facial! Deal?! Yes?!"

I could not believe Miss Bri-Bri was trying to BRIBE me!

She could NEVER buy my SILENCE after completely DESTROYING poor Mrs. Wallabanger's prized flower garden next door!!

Although, that DISCOUNT on a facial DID sound like a pretty good deal!

I LOVE going to the spa and getting those fancy-schmancy treatments. But I digress. . . .

"For your information, spas have ALMOND SCRUB facials! NOT peanut butter facials!" I corrected Miss Bri-Bri. "And PLEASE don't tell me you opened Dad's gallon container of natural no-salt, no-sugar peanut butter that he was saving for his birthday and put it on the dogs' faces?"

"Okay, then! Miss Bri-Bri will NOT tell you she opened zee big birthday bucket of natural peanut butter! But she NEVER, EVER put a drip of zee peanut butter on zee dogs' FACES!" she exclaimed. "What kind of a spa do you think this eez? So please! Do not worry about zat, dah-ling!"

"Thank goodness!" I muttered to myself, and breathed a sigh of relief.

"Today we have a special on zee FULL-BODY peanut butter massage. So I put zee peanut butter ALL OVER zee DOGS' BODIES," Miss Bri-Bri announced proudly. "Now zee dogs eez very relaxed! SEE?"

I looked behind her and gasped!

Holly and her seven puppies were puke brown and covered in peanut butter. . . .

DOGGIES AT THE PAW SPA!

"OMG! What have you done?! These dogs are COMPLETELY covered in Dad's BIRTHDAY peanut butter!!" I shrieked hysterically.

"Bah! Nonsense!" Miss Bri-Bri waved her hand at me dismissively. "I make zee dogs booty-ful. If zee dogs don't look good, I don't look good."

"Admit it, Miss Bri-Bri. You totally screwed up. These dogs look like some furballs that a giant cat coughed up after eating 139 peanut butter cookies," I complained. "Are you even a licensed spa professional?!"

"No need to be rude, dah-ling!" Miss Bri-Bri huffed. "Zee situation eez under control! My spa assistant-in-training, HANS, has prepared a special bath. All zee peanut-butter-covered dogs will be squeaky clean very soon. HANS! Please come clean zee dogs! NOW!"

I couldn't help but roll my eyes when she mentioned her assistant, HANS!

I will NEVER, EVER forget that guy!

Hans the TEDDY BEAR was the assistant on duty at SALON BRIANNA the day Miss Bri-Bri accidentally chopped off my ponytail back in February!

And he's an INCOMPETENT IDIOT!!

But WHATEVER!

Personally, I didn't care if the TOOTH FAIRY was going to help SANTA CLAUS give these dogs a bath.

As long as they were CLEAN, back in their CAGE, and HIDDEN in my room before Mom and Dad got home from the movie!

Miss Bri-Bri and I herded Holly and her puppies into the bathroom to put them into the tub for a quick bath.

That's when I realized we had three very BIG problems:

1. Her poorly trained teddy bear assistant, HANS, was floating upside down in the tub.

2. The tub wasn't filled with water. It was filled with . . .

# MUD?!!!...

AND

3. It wasn't just ordinary mud. The smell of that steaming cesspool was foul enough to peel the baby ducks right off the bathroom wallpaper!

"Brianna! WHY is there MUD in this bathtub?!" I screamed. "And why does it smell like something DIED in the mud and is STILL in there rotting?"

"_Wee! Wee!_ Dis mud eez made of zee finest, filthiest dirt, hand-selected from Mrs. Wallabanger's MANURE compost pile by Miss Bri-Bri herself," she boasted. "You will not find another mud bath like it anywhere in zee world, dah-ling!"

ME, GAGGING AT THE HORRID
STENCH OF MISS BRI-BRI'S
MANURE AND MUD SPA BATH!!

OMG! The hot mud and manure bath smelled so bad, it actually singed my nose hairs.

It was like I could actually TASTE it.

"EWW!!" I gasped, and plugged my nose. "That's it, Brianna! I'm shutting you down!" I yelled. "This pretend spa is CLOSED. Sorry! But this has to be in violation of at least a dozen city health codes!!"

"But, Nikki, I'm NOT finished yet!" ~~Miss Bri-Bri~~ Brianna whined. "After the mud bath, Hans was going to give the dogs a jelly manicure. See?" She held up a jar of grape jelly and a plastic spoon.

"WHAT are you talking about? It's a GEL manicure, NOT a jelly manicure!" I corrected her. "Now get your teddy bear out of this tub so I can clean up this STINKY mess!"

"Hans? HANS!! Get out of that tub or you're FIRED!!" Miss Bri-Bri screamed as she grabbed his leg and tugged on him really hard.

THIS is what happened. . . .

467

OMG! I couldn't believe it! Hans flew across the room like a torpedo and landed headfirst right in the toilet with a huge *SPLASH!*

Of course, Miss Bri-Bri and I totally FREAKED OUT because thanks to Hans, NOW we were dripping with manure and TOILET WATER!

# EWWWWWW ☹!!! . . .

And by the time Brianna and I had chased down the dogs and herded them BACK into their cage, we were covered with manure, toilet water, and PEANUT BUTTER ☹!!

Surprisingly, taking care of the EIGHT dogs has NOT been my most difficult task. It's been taking care of ~~Miss Bri-Bri~~ Brianna!

Sorry, but all night she's been acting like a PACK OF WILD DOGS ☹!!

The last time I checked, Hans was still floating in the toilet. Which wasn't so bad, considering the fact that the toilet was ten times more sanitary than that manure mud bath!!

The dogs were FILTHY.

The bathroom was FILTHY.

And even Brianna and I were FILTHY.

There was just no WAY I could clean up all this FILTH before my parents got home.

Unless they were coming home in two weeks!!

My mom and dad were going to FREAK when they discovered not ONE dog, but EIGHT sticky, peanut-butter-covered dogs hiding inside their FILTHY house!!

I was a complete FAILURE!! And the WORST pet sitter EVER!!

Although, judging from the looks of Brianna, I was probably an even WORSE babysitter ☹!

So I decided to do what any normal responsible teen would do when faced with EIGHT dogs and ONE bratty little sister covered in manure, toilet water, and peanut butter.

I flopped down in the middle of the bathroom floor . . .

Closed my eyes . . .

And burst into TEARS!!

@)!!

I don't know exactly how long I'd been lying on the bathroom floor crying. I just remember hearing the doorbell ringing and wondering three things:

1. Why Mom and Dad were home so early from the movie theater.

2. Why they were ringing the doorbell instead of using their key to the front door.

AND

3. Whether they were going to ground me until my SENIOR year of high school or my FRESHMAN year of college.

Finally, ~~Miss Bri Bri~~ Brianna poked her head in the bathroom and told me what I already knew.

"Nikki, you better come downstairs quick! Someone is at the front door ringing the doorbell!" she

473

exclaimed. "And if it's Mom and Dad, I'm going to go lock myself in my bedroom and play Princess Sugar Plum. But if they're REALLY mad, just tell them I ran away. Okay?"

I could NOT believe Brianna was just going to throw me under the bus like that! This whole thing was HER idea! Miss Bri-Bri's PAW SPA was a HOT MESS!!

*DING-DONG! DING-DONG! DING-DONG!*

JUST GREAT ☹! I could tell Mom and Dad were mad just by the way they were ringing the doorbell.

Still covered in toilet water, manure, and peanut butter, I sadly trudged downstairs to answer the door. All I could really say to my parents was that I was truly sorry, I had learned my lesson, and I would NEVER, EVER lie to them or hide anything from them AGAIN!!

I slowly opened the front door and was completely shocked to see . . .

474

# . . . BRANDON?!

"BRANDON!! OMG! WHAT are you doing here?"
I gasped.

"Nikki, are you okay?" he asked, looking panicked. "I called your cell to see how things were going with the dogs. And, well . . . this really weird lady with a thick accent answered. She said you couldn't come to the phone because you were really mad about the peanut butter and mud and you were crying in the bathroom! She said something about hands being in the toilet and you closing her pa's spa! None of it made any sense! And then she just HUNG UP on me! It was so . . . BIZARRE!"

"WHAT?!" I sputtered.

I was SHOCKED! Brianna had actually answered MY cell phone and TALKED to Brandon?!!

I could NOT believe that girl was putting ALL my personal business in the STREETS like that!

Brandon continued. "I thought I had the wrong number, so I called back again. The same lady answered and told me not to call her again or she was contacting the cops. Anyway, since I was

476

right in the neighborhood working on a project, I thought I'd just drop by to make sure everything was okay! You and the dogs ARE okay, right?! That lady really had me worried. And, um . . . what's that SMELL?! PEW!!" he said, blinking his eyes really fast like the odor was stinging them or something.

Sorry, but I was NOT about to tell Brandon the truth. That he had trusted me with the dogs and I was a COMPLETE and UTTER FAILURE as a pet sitter ☹!

So I decided to just LIE about how I'd read in *Teen Thing* magazine that washing dogs in peanut butter and manure compost killed all fleas (within ten miles!) and gave them really shiny coats.

And yes! It had turned out to be a bit messier than I had anticipated.

So I was in the process of cleaning (the dogs, my little sister, Hans the teddy bear, and half of the entire upstairs).

Then I decided to change the subject.

"So, Brandon, you said you were in the neighborhood?"

"Yeah. I was actually right next door in the white house. My good friend Max Crumbly and I are working on our project for the science fair. It's due tomorrow."

"That house?" I asked, surprised. "You were at Mrs. Wallabanger's?!"

"Yeah, Mrs. Wallabanger is Max's grandmother! Our project is called Using Distillation to Turn Dirty Water into Clean Drinking Water."

"Wow, Brandon! Our bio teacher mentioned the science fair. Your project sounds really complicated."

"Actually, it's not. It involves taking dirty water and turning it into clean drinking water. With enough research, one day this process could help provide clean water to Third World nations. Anyway, for our project to work, we need to use dirty water occurring naturally in the environment."

"That's totally amazing!" I gushed.

"We planned to use dirty runoff water from Mrs. Wallabanger's compost pile. But we just discovered that it's gone. So it looks like we might not be entering the science fair after all."

"Wow! What happened?" I asked, concerned.

"I know it sounds hard to believe, but it looks like someone vandalized her backyard and stole her compost. They also took a few of her prized flowers. Max's grandma insists her archfrenemy, Trixie Claire Jewel-Hollister, is behind it. They've been rivals since high school. Mrs. Wallabanger has been winning first place in all the local flower shows lately, and she says Trixie Hollister is a rich, spoiled, jealous SORE LOSER."

I was almost sure that Hollister lady was probably MacKenzie's grandmother or grandaunt.

I felt bad they were blaming her, but I didn't want to throw Brianna under the bus either.

"Well, I'm really sorry to hear you and Max might not be entering the science fair because— Wait a minute! I think I just might have some manure—I mean, COMPOST—lying around that I don't need!"

Brandon looked surprised. "You do?! Really?! Wow, that's great news! Can we borrow some for our project?"

"Actually, you can have ALL of it! I was planning to get rid of it anyway. But I'll need a little help, if you guys don't mind."

So I cleaned the FILTHY TOILET.

Brandon cleaned the FILTHY BATHTUB (he really liked Miss Bri-Bri's "SPA MUD").

And his friend Max cleaned the FILTHY DOGS in Mrs. Wallabanger's backyard. . . .

MAX, GIVING HOLLY AND
THE PUPPIES A BATH!

Brandon introduced me to his good friend Max Crumbly. He was nice, friendly, smart, and, ALMOST as CUTE as Brandon! SQUEEEE ☺!!

NIKKI, MEET MY GOOD FRIEND MAX CRUMBLY! HE'S MRS. WALLABANGER'S GRANDSON!

Brandon said Max is a really good artist (like ME!) and attends South Ridge public middle school just down the street.

They both thanked me for helping them out with their science project and invited me to attend.

Anyway, by the time my parents got home from the movie, everything and everyone was squeaky clean and fast asleep!

Yes, I admit that the evening was a COMPLETE DISASTER!!

WHY did I EVER think I could take care of EIGHT dogs when I could barely keep a PET ROCK alive?!

But, in the end, everything worked out just fine!

Maybe Miss Bri-Bri's full-body peanut butter massage DID relax the dogs. They've been quiet as mice all night.

I just hope tomorrow will be a lot less DRAMA!

Mom and Dad are chaperoning an all-day field trip to the Westchester Zoo for Brianna's class. So the three of them will already be gone by the time I get up.

I'll just let the dogs romp, play, and nap in my bedroom (with their pee-pee mat) until I get home from school.

THEN, by the time my family is back from the field trip, Brandon will have picked up the dogs and taken them to Chloe's house, and my pet sitting duties will be successfully completed!

Which means I will have kept EIGHT dogs right under my parents' noses for twenty-four hours without them EVER suspecting a thing!

Am I NOT an EVIL GENIUS?!

# MWA-HA-HA-HA!

Well, I'd better get some sleep!

☺!!

# AAAAAAAAAAAAAAAH!!!

(That was me screaming in TERROR!)

At first I didn't know if I was actually dreaming or awake. I was praying the very horrible THING I saw was just a really bad nightmare!

I had awakened, showered, and gotten dressed. Then I'd taken care of Holly and her pups.

They were in my room playing and romping around when I went downstairs to grab breakfast and head off to school.

WARNING! This is the scary NIGHTMARE part!

Just like the ~~victims~~ people in those horror movies, I was supposed to be home alone!

So, I totally FREAKED when I walked into the kitchen and saw . . .

ME, IN SHOCK MOM IS STILL HOME,
WHEN SHE WAS SUPPOSED TO BE GONE!

I was like, "Um, good morning, Mom! So . . .
WHAT ARE YOU DOING HERE?!!"

Mom looked at me kind of strange. "Well, right now
I'm making a cup of coffee."

"What I meant was, aren't you and Dad supposed
to be gone all day? You know, chaperoning Brianna's
class at the zoo?"

"Actually, it was canceled due to a forecast of
thundershowers. And since I've already taken
the time off from work, I decided to just stay
home and relax."

"WHAT?! You're staying HOME?!! ALL DAY?!
Are you SURE?!" I gasped.

"Yes, I'm sure! Honey, are you feeling okay? You kind
of look like you just saw a GHOST or something!"

"Actually, Mom, I felt just fine until I walked
into this kitchen. Now I wanna throw up! Er, what

I mean is . . . YES! I'm not sick at all. And I'm feeling very fine, actually," I babbled.

Okay, I had a HUMONGOUS problem!

There was no way I could leave the dogs in my bedroom with Mom in the house all day.

And even if I stashed them in the garage, she'd probably stumble upon them out there, too.

I needed to get them out of the house, and FAST!!

If one of the puppies even SNEEZED, there was a good chance Mom would hear it, all alone in the house with eight dogs ☹!

Unlike my SCHOOL, which was busy, crowded, and practically a ZOO!

That place was usually so NOISY, I could BARELY hear my own THOUGHTS!

As crazy as it sounded, I didn't have a choice but
to take the dogs to SCHOOL with me!!

Or face the WRATH OF MOM ☹!!

I texted Chloe and Zoey and made them aware
of the impending CATASTROPHE!

They told me to remain calm and meet them at
the side door near the school library ASAP.

But I STILL had to resolve TWO very minor,
yet important, questions.

Since no one orders pizzas for breakfast at 7:00 a.m.,
Queasy Cheesy was still closed and their drivers were
not available. So HOW was I supposed to convince my
mom or dad to drive me and EIGHT dogs to school?
Without them EVER discovering the, um, DOGS?

That's when I suddenly remembered that my BFFs
and I were meeting near the LIBRARY. And it had
lots and lots of BOOKS.

So I grabbed a marker, paper, blanket, and wagon and created the perfect doggie disguise. . . .

I had barely finished covering the dog cage with Brianna's old baby blanket when I suddenly heard the garage door open.

Brianna's eyes got as big as saucers, and she looked like she was about to wet her pants.

When I turned around, Dad was standing there with a mug of coffee, STARING right at the DOG CAGE.

OMG! I was SO startled, I almost lost my biscuits-'n'-gravy breakfast.

Dad looked at the dog cage and then at me and then back at the dog cage again. I thought for sure I was BUSTED!!

Until he said, "So, Nikki, it looks like you're going to need help getting those library books to school. I'll go unlock the van and load you up."

I was speechless. And very happy ☺!!

My dad had volunteered to take me and the ~~dogs~~ "library books" to school!

"Thanks, Dad," I said. "I really appreciate it."

"That's a BIG load of books! Where did you find them, Nikki?" he asked, taking a swig of coffee.

"Actually, someone left them all on a doorstep, and I've been taking care of them until I could find them a home. Well, A HOME in our school LIBRARY, of course!" I explained nervously.

Dad unlocked the van door and went back into the house to let Mom know he was driving me to school.

I quickly wheeled the "books" out to the van, and Brianna helped me load everything inside before he returned.

As Dad pulled out of the driveway, I turned on the radio and blasted his favorite golden oldies music station so loud I thought my ears were going to bleed.

Luckily, the loud music made it almost impossible for Dad to hear the dogs bark.

BUT if he had glanced at the "library books" behind him, he would have been in for a really big surprise. . . .

My heart was pounding in my chest like the bass to my favorite rap song as I adjusted the blanket to cover the curious puppies.

# WHAT WAS I THINKING ☹?!!

I must have been suffering from TEMPORARY INSANITY when I came up with the RIDICULOUS idea to bring eight dogs to school.

I was already DREADING my day at school!

And it hadn't even started yet.

☹!!

As planned, Chloe and Zoey were waiting for me by the side door near the library.

"Hi, guys!" I jumped out of the van, grabbed their arms, and led them to the back of the van so Dad couldn't hear.

"So, will you help me unload the, um . . . BOOKS?!"

"Books?" Zoey asked. "What books?"

I gave her and Chloe a wink.

"Oh! THOSE books! Sure!" Zoey said.

"Nikki, what happened to the DOGS?" Chloe blurted out. "Are they still in your bedroom?! I thought you were bringing them with you to school today and—

Zoey gave Chloe a swift kick to shut her up.

"OW! That hurt!" Chloe whined.

"Need any help, girls?" Dad asked, standing right behind us.

OMG! He nearly scared the Kibbles 'n Bits out of us! I really wished he'd STOP sneaking up on people like that.

He opened the back door of the van and reached for the load of "library books."

"NO!" I said, grabbing his hand. "I mean, no thanks, Dad! We got this. Mrs. Peach would fire us from working at the library. You understand, right?"

"Not really. But fine." He shrugged. "You kids are more nervous than a wet cat! It's like you're trying to smuggle mice into a cheese factory or something!"

Not quite! We were trying to smuggle eight dogs into a middle school.

496

Chloe, Zoey, and I looked at each other and giggled nervously.

Not because his joke was funny, but because Holly's tail was hanging out from under the blanket. . . .

After Chloe, Zoey, and I unloaded the dog cage and wagon, we waved good-bye to my dad, and wheeled the "books" into the library.

"Keeping the cage in here might be risky!" I said, looking around. "What if Mrs. Peach sees the sign and thinks it's actually library books?"

"Maybe if we change the sign to 'GARBAGE,' she won't look?" Chloe reasoned. "But then she might throw it out. I know! How about 'SNAKES'? Then she wouldn't go near it!"

"No! We should hide the dogs in a safe, top secret place that only WE know about. Like, hmmm . . . ," Zoey said, tapping her chin.

Suddenly we all had the exact same idea. . . .

"THE JANITOR'S CLOSET!" we yelled excitedly.

We quickly wheeled the cage down the hall to the janitor's closet. . . .

We rolled the cage inside and closed the door.

"I just hope the dogs aren't too noisy," Zoey said, pulling off the blanket and folding it up.

"Well, we can listen to them with this," I said, reaching inside my backpack and pulling out the baby monitor.

Chloe turned it on and placed the receiver part on top of the cage and handed the speaker part to me.

All the puppies were resting, and Holly quietly stared out at us, probably curious about her strange new surroundings.

"Look!" Chloe said. "Her water bowl is empty. I'll fill it back up so she won't get thirsty!"

"Okay, but just make sure you close the cage when you're done so they can't get out," I said, turning the volume on the receiver to high.

I wanted to make sure I could hear every little sound. Then I placed it inside my backpack.

We said good-bye to the dogs, carefully closed the janitor's closet door, and headed for our lockers.

Today, students were reporting to their homerooms for first hour instead of our regular classes.

This worked out for us since we were all in the same homeroom.

"Whatever you do, act natural and stay cool," I whispered to Chloe and Zoey as we took our seats.

"And just think POSITIVE thoughts!" Zoey whispered.

"Yeah, because if someone finds those dogs in the janitor's closet, I'm POSITIVE we'll be KICKED

out of this school like a SOCCER BALL!" Chloe
added in a whisper.

I was like, thanks a lot, Chloe!

After hearing her positive thought, I was more
WORRIED than EVER!!

☹!!

The classroom was so quiet, you could hear a pin drop. Then . . .

# BOOM! SPLASH! BARK! YIP-YIP! CRASH!

The loud noises from my backpack startled me so badly I practically jumped out of my seat. OMG! It sounded like pure puppy pandemonium!

I immediately regretted that I'd turned up the volume of the baby monitor so high.

I ALSO immediately regretted that I hadn't checked to make sure Chloe had CLOSED that CAGE DOOR after refilling Holly's water bowl ☹!!

Every single person in the room heard it, including Chloe and Zoey. I totally panicked.

My startled teacher stopped writing on the board, walked over to my desk, and gawked at me. . . .

ME, DISRUPTING THE CLASS WITH MY
VERY NOISY "STOMACH SOUNDS"

"Nikki, are you okay?!" she asked, looking very concerned.

"Uh . . . have you ever been so queasy that your stomach sounds like seven dogs fighting in a utility closet?! That's totally me right now!" I grabbed my stomach and faked a very loud and painful moan.

My teacher shuddered at the thought.

"Actually, no, I haven't. Thankfully!" she muttered.

YIP-YIP! BANG! SQUEAL! BARK! CRASH!

"Sorry! But this could get really ugly!" I said, and then moaned really long and loud like a moose with a bad toothache.

Mostly I was trying my hardest to cover up the noise coming from my backpack.

But I don't think it was working.

"I'm really worried about you, Nikki! Did you maybe eat something that didn't agree with you?!" my teacher asked.

"Probably! Remember that blue cheese macaroni casserole from lunch yesterday? Only it was actually more of a moldy green color and smelled like fermented skunk spit? I ate THREE large bowls of it! UGH!!"

I watched as kids frantically scooted their desks out of my puking range.

Come on! Even if I really had eaten that stuff, they wouldn't need to move away like that.

Hey! They'd need to SWIM out of the room!

I'm just sayin'.

SQUEAL! BARK! CRASH! YIP-YIP! BANG! GRRRR! BARK! YIP! CRASH! BANG! CRASH!

A few kids were staring at me in horror, like I was possessed! By the DRUM SECTION of a small middle school MARCHING BAND!

What were those dogs doing in there?

Chasing BOWLING BALLS?! And playing fetch with the MOP BUCKETS?!

"OW! OW! OOOOOOW!" Zoey suddenly yelled like a coyote howling at the moon. "Teacher, I had too much of that MOLD-A-RONI—er, I mean, macaroni—too! I am SOOOO sick!"

Then Chloe joined in. "MOO! QUACK-QUACK! OINK-OINK! COCK-A-DOODLE-DOO!!"

Girlfriend was definitely overdoing the theatrics. She sounded like a barnyard at sunrise!

Then, for dramatic effect, I reenacted that infamous scene from that time MacKenzie threw up in French class!! . . .

CHLOE, ZOEY, AND ME,
PRETENDING TO BE VERY SICK!

OMG! That's when the entire classroom went completely nuts!

Everyone knows that puking can be contagious. It's probably never BEEN scientifically proven, but STILL!

At least four other kids were holding their mouths and starting to look really sick too.

Only, unlike Chloe, Zoey, and ME, THOSE kids were probably REALLY going to THROW UP ☹!!

Just one kid getting sick in class was SUPERgross!

# EWW!!

But FOUR at the same time?!

## Quadruple EWW!!

I definitely didn't want to be around when THAT happened.

"OH NO!" my teacher cried, suddenly realizing the gravity of the situation. "All three of you are IMMEDIATELY excused! Now HURRY, before your lunch comes back to say hello all over my clean floor! GO! Please! Just GO!"

It was quite clear the teacher had heard about the MACKENZIE PUKE FIASCO. Because THIS lady was NOT having it in HER classroom!!

Chloe, Zoey, and I exchanged glances.

In spite of our very bad acting skills, our plan was obviously working!

"Tank you, Teacher!" I grimaced.

Then I grabbed my backpack, and the three of us staggered out of the room all queasylike.

But as soon as I closed the door, we sprinted down the hall toward the janitor's closet like we were competing in a 100-meter dash. . . .

CHLOE, ZOEY, AND ME, RACING DOWN
THE HALL TO CHECK ON THE DOGS!

As we sprinted down the hall, it felt like the janitor's closet was two miles away.

By the time we reached it, we were pretty frantic and completely out of breath.

I cautiously opened the door, and the three of us peeked in.

# OMG!

I couldn't believe the **HUGE** mess those dogs had made!

It gave a whole new meaning to that popular old-school song "WHO LET THE DOGS OUT"!

But mostly, we couldn't believe all the FUN the puppies seemed to be having.

Everything in there had been . . .

Chewed.

Gnawed.

Chipped.

Scratched.

Torn.

Tattered.

Shattered.

Shredded.

Or broken.

# But thank goodness!!

The DOGS were all in one piece and doing just fine. . . .

TOILET
PAPER

TOILET
PAPER

TOILET
PAPER

TOILET
PAPER

There were mounds of powdered detergent, puddles of dirty mop water, soap suds, and shredded toilet paper everywhere! Two puppies were playing with the water hose in the mop sink.

I'm no dog whisperer, but I think Holly was totally embarrassed by her puppies' antics.

It was hard to believe that such LITTLE puppies could make such a HUMONGOUS mess. It actually looked like they'd thrown a wild house party in there and TRASHED the place!

"It's going to take at least an hour to clean this mess up," Zoey groaned. "We'll just have to come back and tackle it during lunch when we have more time."

"Yeah, I know. But we need to get the dogs out of here first," I muttered.

"Where else can we put them?" Chloe asked. "Mrs. Peach will be in the library all afternoon, so THAT'S not an option!"

"Guys! I have a REALLY CRAZY idea." I grinned.
"And I'm pretty sure it will probably work!
Or WRECK our lives and get us EXPELLED
from school."

"Wow, sounds just perfect!" Zoey replied
sarcastically, and rolled her eyes.

"Just hear me out," I said. "Principal Winston is
out of the building all day today for a meeting
at the high school. Right?! Well, since he's not
in his office—"

"I know!" Chloe interrupted excitedly. "We can just
SKIP SCHOOL for the rest of the day and take
the dogs to MY house! Since he's not here, he won't
know and we won't get EXPELLED! Right?!"

"Not exactly, Chloe. Just LISTEN, okay?" I said,
mildly annoyed. "We could hide the dogs in his office,
and no one would EVER find them. That's because
absolutely no one would even DARE go in there
without his permission. Unless they were REALLY,
REALLY STUPID or something!!"

Zoey slapped her palm on her forehead. "DUH!! Am I the ONLY one who sees the IRONY here? Sheesh!"

"There's an IRON in here?!" Chloe asked, looking around. "Where is it? Like, who would iron clothes in a janitor's closet? Oooh! I know! The JANITOR, right?"

"Chloe! I said 'IRONY'!" Zoey sighed.

"I know. I heard you the first time. But I still don't see any iron," Chloe muttered.

"Chloe! There's NO iron! Trust me," I said.

"I didn't THINK so! Tell that to Zoey," Chloe grumped.

"Come on, Zoey!" I argued. "If you have a better idea, let's hear it."

"Actually, I think Chloe's really stupid idea of SKIPPING school is BETTER. And LESS risky," she grumbled.

I just rolled my eyes at Zoey and didn't say a word.

Finally Zoey sighed. "Nikki, if you think your plan will actually work, let's try it! We definitely CAN'T keep the dogs in here!"

"Great!" I smiled. "Now, listen carefully, guys. My plan is VERY, VERY simple! ALL we have to do is SNEAK the dogs into Principal Winston's office, keep them from totally TRASHING the place like they did the janitor's closet, make sure no one accidentally discovers them, and then SNEAK back into his office at the end of the day and take them home! Like, how hard can THAT BE?!"

Chloe and Zoey just folded their arms and stared at me.

"So that's the plan. Do you guys have any questions?" I asked happily.

"Yes, I think Chloe and I have the same question," Zoey muttered. . . .

Okay, I wasn't quite expecting THAT question. But hey, that's Chloe and Zoey. You gotta LOVE 'EM!

## FRIDAY—8:43 A.M.
## IN THE SCHOOL OFFICE

Coming up with the idea to hide the dogs in Principal Winston's office was pretty easy.

However, figuring out HOW to get the dogs into Principal Winston's office was the hard part. So this was the MASTER PLAN!

Chloe was going to lock herself in a bathroom stall and ~~do her very bad imitations of various barnyard animals~~ pretend to be sick.

We'd ask the office secretary to check on Chloe because we were worried about her.

While the secretary was out of the office, Zoey and I would simply roll the dog cage into Principal Winston's office and close his door.

Since his office was in a separate corridor from the noisy main office, it would be pretty hard to hear the dogs unless they made a huge racket.

Then, at the end of the day, we'd simply ask to retrieve our box of "library books" that had inadvertently ended up in Principal Winston's office instead of in the library.

I knew my plan was far-fetched, ill-conceived, and very risky. But I didn't have any other options.

Except to confess everything to my parents ☹!

We were scoping out the office when the door opened and the secretary walked down the hall and disappeared into the teachers' lounge.

We couldn't believe our good luck ☺!

With the office temporarily unattended, we'd have the PERFECT opportunity to sneak the dogs into the principal's office.

We grabbed the wagon and rushed into the office, only to discover some GOOD news and some BAD news. The BAD news was that there was a student office assistant on duty ☹!

But the GOOD news was that it was our friend
MARCY ☺!! . . .

OUR GOOD FRIEND MARCY IS THE STUDENT
OFFICE ASSISTANT ON DUTY!

"What's up, Marcy?" I said. "We have a really big favor we'd like to ask you! It's kind of a secret!"

She stared at the wagon behind us with a puzzled look on her face. Then she read the sign and blinked in disbelief.

"OMG! I can't believe you guys would actually do something like this! And you expect me to keep it a secret?! The entire school needs to know what you're doing!" Marcy screeched excitedly.

It seemed really clear from her over-the-top reaction that she must have spotted a puppy peeking out from under the blanket, or a wayward tail wagging or something.

JUST GREAT! We were so BUSTED ☹!!

Chloe, Zoey, and I went into panic mode.

"Listen, Marcy, I can explain all of this! Just give me a chance! Please!" I pleaded with her.

"When the secretary returns from her break, I'm sure she's going to be as shocked and surprised by what you're doing as I am! Of course she'll inform Principal Winston the minute he gets back," Marcy continued.

"Actually, Marcy, it looks like you're pretty busy here. So we really should be getting back to class!" Zoey exclaimed. "Have a nice day!"

But Chloe totally lost it.

"OH NO!! Now we're going to get EXPELLED from school and our parents are going to KILL us!!" she shrieked hysterically as she grabbed her stomach. "UGH! I think I'm going to be SICK! For real! Cock-a-doodle-doo! Moo! Oink!"

"Okay, Marcy, I won't bother to explain what we're trying to do! So just forget we were even here!" I said in frustration.

"No! You don't have to explain anything. It's quite obvious. You're collecting book donations for the library! AGAIN! Right?! You guys are unbelievable! Our school is really lucky to have dedicated students like you so willing to give of yourselves. Principal Winston should give each of you the Student of the Year award! I'M just SO proud and honored to be your friend!" Marcy gushed.

"NOW, WHAT CAN I DO TO HELP?!"

Chloe, Zoey, and I glanced at each other and giggled nervously.

WHEW!! That was close!

I was glad Marcy had offered to help us.

But after her glowing compliments, asking her to ABUSE her position as student office assistant by helping us smuggle eight dogs into Principal Winston's office had suddenly gotten a lot harder!

I had chosen to get involved in all of this to try to help Brandon save Holly and her puppies.

But to involve innocent people like my BFFs, and now Marcy!

I felt like a SNAKE! A dishonest, manipulative, and very DESPERATE snake!

I didn't have a choice but to call my parents and tell them everything. BEFORE I got my friends and myself into serious trouble.

"Thanks, Marcy! So does this mean we're NOT getting EXPELLED for sneaking Holly and her puppies into school?!" Chloe blurted out.

Zoey gave Chloe a swift kick to shut her up.

"OW! That hurt!" Chloe grumped, and shot Zoey a dirty look.

"Puppies?! Did you just say PUPPIES?!" Marcy gasped excitedly. "OMG! I LOVE puppies! I've been begging my parents to get one, like, FOREVER! Where are they?! Can I see them?! PLEEEEEEASE!!"

Okay, that's when I decided NOT to call my parents and tell them about Holly and her puppies.

S-s-so what if I'm a s-s-s-sneaky s-s-s-snake ☺!

I told Marcy all about Holly and her pups and how we were helping Brandon save them.

Then I let her have a peek at them. . . .

ME, SHOWING MARCY THE DOGS!!

Marcy didn't seem the least bit disappointed that
our library books were actually dogs.

And after hearing about our doggie dilemma, Marcy agreed that Principal Winston's office would make the PERFECT hideout until the end of the school day ☺!!

Especially since Principal Winston wasn't expected to return during school hours.

"Marcy, we really appreciate you offering to help, but are you SURE you want to do this?! If we get caught, you could get detention—or worse!" I warned her.

"Well, to be honest, I'm not that worried about detention. I just don't want to be demoted from office assistant to team uniform assistant. The sweaty guys on our wrestling team are the worst! After practice their uniforms smell like Dumpster juice and swamp gas!" she complained. "ICK!!"

"Marcy, we totally understand if you're having second thoughts about helping us," I said sympathetically.

"Yeah, we wouldn't ask you to do something this crazy and risky unless it was for a really good cause," Zoey explained.

But Chloe was no help whatsoever. She made a sad pouty face like she was about to cry.

"Marcy, just look at these cute wittle faces!" Chloe squeaked in baby talk. "Don't you just wuv these wittle doggies! Yes, you willy do!"

Almost as if on cue, all eight dogs gave us the biggest, saddest, most angelic puppy-dog eyes EVER!

"Awwwwww!" the four of us gushed.

"Poor wittle puppies are willy, willy sad!" Chloe said glumly.

"Okay, guys! I'm in!" Marcy sniffed. "I'd have to be completely HEARTLESS to say no to those cute wittle faces. I already wuv 'em! I willy do!"

531

Chloe, Zoey, and I were so happy, we gave Marcy a group hug!

"Thanks, guys!" Marcy smiled. "The secretary will be coming back from her break any minute now. We need to get these dogs moved into Principal Winston's office right away!"

I guess the fact that we were ACTUALLY about to hide eight dogs in the principal's office must have FINALLY sunk in or something.

Because suddenly my heart started to pound. And my palms got SUPERsweaty. And my stomach started to feel very queasy for real!

I took a deep breath, nodded, and calmly said, "Okay, Marcy, let's do this!"

But inside my head I was totally FREAKING OUT!

I wanted to run out of the office hysterically screaming. . . .

I just hope my KA-RAY-ZEE plan actually works!

☹!!

Marcy cautiously turned the knob to Principal Winston's office and . . .

# CLICK!!

OMG! We nearly jumped out of our skins!

"AAAH!!" Chloe shrieked, and grabbed my arm.

Okay, so THAT was the LOUDEST doorknob click EVER!

But STILL!

There was no need for Chloe to act like she'd just seen an ax murderer or something.

"CHLOE! Let go of my arm!" I whisper-shouted.

"Sorry!" she muttered. "I'm just a little jumpy, okay?"

The four of us nervously tiptoed into the dark office, wheeling the dog cage behind us.

For some reason, it felt really creepy in there.

Like at any second some nightmarish creature was going to crawl out of the shadows, grab us with its long, bony claws, and do something really HORRIBLE to us!

You know, like . . .

ENROLL US IN SUMMER SCHOOL!!

# EEEEEEEEEK ☹!!!

Marcy stopped in the middle of the room. "SHHHHH!! Do you guys hear that sound?!"

I definitely heard it!

# KNOCK-KNOCK!

# KNOCK-KNOCK!

"OH NO!" Zoey gasped. "I think someone is knocking on the door! We're DOOMED!"

"That's not the door! It's Chloe's KNEES!!" I said, rolling my eyes.

"Hey, I already told you I was a little jumpy!" Chloe snarked. "This place feels like a haunted house or something! Does anyone have a flashlight?"

"That's it! I can't handle this!" Marcy cried. "I'm going to do what I should've done in the beginning!"

She turned and headed straight for the door.

I could NOT believe she would just panic and abandon us like that.

"Wait, Marcy! Come back!" I whisper-shouted.

"Well, it looks like she'd rather smell funky wrestler uniforms than hang out with us puppy smugglers!" Chloe grumbled. "TRAITOR!"

CHLOE, ZOEY, AND I FREAK OUT AS
MARCY HEADS FOR THE DOOR!

When Marcy reached the door, she stopped.

Then she hit a switch on the wall, and bright lights flooded the room.

Chloe, Zoey, and I blinked in surprise.

"There! Isn't this a lot better?" Marcy said as she opened the curtains on a window. "I don't know about you guys, but the darkness was giving me SERIOUS goose bumps!"

Chloe's fright subsided as we looked around.

The office was a lot less Temple of Doom-looking with the lights on.

Actually, it was kind of on the boring side.

Cheesy-looking certificates hung on the walls, a bookcase was filled with dusty books, and a clock sat next to a framed family photo. A big candy jar sat on his desk along with stacks of papers.

I couldn't help but shudder. Hopefully, today was the FIRST and the LAST time I'd be hanging out in the principal's office.

I folded the doggie blanket and placed it in the wagon.

All the dogs had cuddled together and were about to take their midmorning nap.

"I think they're still exhausted from that big party they had in the janitor's closet. So they'll probably just sleep the rest of the day. You won't even know they're here," I assured Marcy.

"Great! I'll come back to check on them every hour between classes. And if there's a problem, I'll text you, Nikki," Marcy explained. "Otherwise, just meet me here after school to pick them up."

"Thanks, Marcy! You're a lifesaver!" I said.

Suddenly Marcy froze.

"SHHHHHHH!! I hear another strange sound!" she whispered.

# SMACK-SMACK! SMACK! SMACK! SMACK-SMACK!

I definitely heard it too!

Alarmed, Marcy, Zoey, and I stared at the door.

Were those footsteps?

OMG! What if the secretary was coming in to place Principal Winston's mail on his desk and discovered us in here?

I quickly searched the room for a hiding spot.

"Maybe we should hide in that closet!" I shouted quietly.

"Hey, guys! Don't FREAK OUT! It's just ME," Chloe giggled.

We turned around to see her smacking loudly on the last few pieces of chocolate in Principal Winston's candy jar. . . .

CHLOE, SNARFING DOWN CANDY
FROM PRINCIPAL WINSTON'S CANDY JAR!

"Sorry if I sound like a pig! But those mini candy bar thingies are DELISH!"

Evidently, in the sixty seconds we had our backs turned, Chloe had somehow crammed most of the candy bars from that big candy jar into her dainty little mouth!

Seriously! How did she do that?

Does her jaw UNHINGE when she eats, like those huge snakes on the Animal Planet TV shows?!

Anyway, in spite of Chloe's noisy feeding frenzy, the dogs had finally fallen asleep.

Marcy turned out the lights, and we rushed back to the main office.

And just in time, too.

As we headed into the hall on our way to class, the secretary held the door open for us.

"Have a nice day, girls!" She smiled.

"You too!" we said, and smiled back at her.

Anyway, thank goodness the dogs are safely hidden away in Principal Winston's office, where no one will find them.

Now all I have to do is just survive the rest of the school day, which is about FIVE hours.

How HARD can THAT be?!

Chloe, Zoey, and I gobbled down our lunches as fast as we could.

Then we snuck out of the cafeteria and rushed straight to the janitor's closet as planned.

OMG! The room looked like it had been hit by a Category 3 hurricane.

It seemed like it was going to take us FOREVER to clean up the HUGE mess those dogs had made. Although my BFFs and I HATED cleaning our bedrooms and LOATHED putting dishes in the dishwasher, we somehow managed to finish up by the time lunch was over.

How?!

We donned our rubber gloves and combined our strength to become the powerful SUPERHEROES known as . . .

544

Unfortunately for us, we also ended up SMELLING like the janitor's closet ☹!

Which is a combination of soap, toilet bowl cleaner, and musty, moldy MOP!

EWW ☹!!

Anyway, Marcy has been checking on the dogs every hour between classes, and she said she'd text me if anything came up. I haven't heard from her, so NO news is GOOD news ☺!

Maybe this whole dog sitting thing is going to work out after all.

Just a few more hours left until the end of the school day.

# SQUEEEEE!!!
☺!!

FRIDAY—1:00 P.M.
IN BIOLOGY CLASS

The big science fair is today after school, and students are already setting up in the gym. My bio teacher had a flyer posted on her wall. . . .

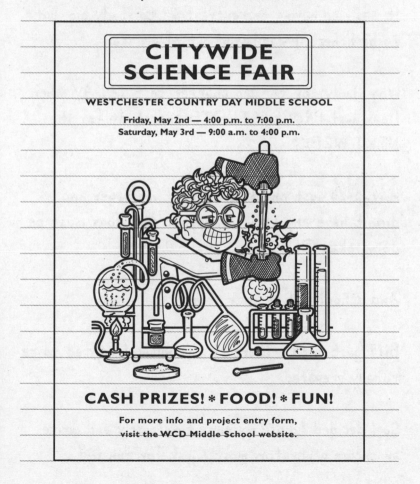

**CITYWIDE SCIENCE FAIR**

WESTCHESTER COUNTRY DAY MIDDLE SCHOOL

Friday, May 2nd — 4:00 p.m. to 7:00 p.m.
Saturday, May 3rd — 9:00 a.m. to 4:00 p.m.

**CASH PRIZES! * FOOD! * FUN!**

For more info and project entry form,
visit the WCD Middle School website.

Since half of the students in our biology class were in the gym setting up for the fair (including Brandon ☺!), our teacher told us we could spend the hour quietly reviewing for our chapter test next week.

It was nice having the extra time to study bio, but to be honest, I was bored out of my skull.

Why study for the bio chapter test TODAY when I can just PROCRASTINATE and study for it NEXT WEEK?

Anyway, I just checked my text messages and didn't have any from Marcy, so the dogs must be doing okay ☺!

And school will be over soon!

BUT just in case there IS a problem, I wanted to be totally prepared.

So I decided to use my class time wisely and write an excuse generator, mostly just for fun ☺!! . . .

# EXCUSE GENERATOR
## FOR WHY THERE ARE EIGHT DOGS
## IN PRINCIPAL WINSTON'S OFFICE

To: Principal Winston

From: Nikki J. Maxwell

Dear Principal Winston,

You are probably wondering why there are eight dogs in your office. So, please, allow me to explain.

But first, I sincerely want you to know that I'm just as:

- ☐ shocked
- ☐ confused
- ☐ hungry
- ☐ bald

as you are about this very troubling situation.

I was on my way to class this morning when
I thought I heard:

- ☐ scratching
- ☐ barfing
- ☐ singing
- ☐ "cock-a-doodle-doo"

at one of the exit doors.

I assumed it was just:

- ☐ a pizza delivery guy
- ☐ a circus clown
- ☐ a rabid squirrel
- ☐ a bloodthirsty vampire

trying to get in.

So I opened the door just a tiny bit to get
a quick peek. But before I could stop them,
eight dogs quickly ran inside.

I tried to catch them, but they were faster than:
- ☐ lightning
- ☐ uncontrolled diarrhea
- ☐ a slug in an ice storm
- ☐ a race car driver with four flat tires

and they somehow disappeared down a hallway.

So I thoroughly searched every single:
- ☐ classroom
- ☐ toilet
- ☐ locker
- ☐ garbage Dumpster

but I STILL couldn't find them.

This made me so frustrated that I wanted to:
- ☐ eat a peanut butter, jelly, and pickle sandwich

☐ pick my nose
☐ do the hokey pokey
☐ take a bubble bath

and then sob hysterically.

The only place I HADN'T searched was your
office! And that was because I didn't want to
break any school rules and possibly risk getting:
☐ expelled from WCD
☐ an after-school detention
☐ a severe case of diaper rash
☐ a zit on my nose the size of a raisin

which, unfortunately, would become part
of my permanent school record and possibly
prevent me from getting admitted to a
major university.

Sadly, I had no choice but to search for
the dogs in your office.

Of course, as soon as I found them there,
I immediately:
- ☐ wet my pants
- ☐ fainted
- ☐ took a selfie
- ☐ stepped in doggie poo

which was such a traumatic experience that
it will take me years to recover.

Fortunately, the dogs were merely:
- ☐ eating student report cards
- ☐ drinking out of the toilet
- ☐ chewing a hole in your leather office
  chair
- ☐ taking a nap

so your office was not heavily damaged.

I had just left your office to call Fuzzy
Friends Animal Rescue Center to pick up

the dogs and find them homes, when I
discovered you had returned and found the
dogs in your office.

I'll never again open our school doors for:
☐ eight renegade retrievers
☐ seven prissy poodles
☐ six yappy Yorkies
☐ five dorky Dalmatians and a partridge
  in a pear tree

because I have learned my lesson.

Sincerely,

NIKKI J. MAXWELL

☺!

It's hard to believe a day that started so HORRIBLY WRONG is ending so PERFECTLY RIGHT ☺!

Chloe, Zoey, and I were working in the library as LSAs (library shelving assistants) when Brandon stopped by.

We both had been really busy with stuff and hadn't seen each other all day.

"Hey, Nikki! I just wanted to thank you again for that compost for my science project. I gave the leftovers to Mrs. Wallabanger, and she was thrilled. She plans to use it to fix her flower garden."

"No problem! I'm always happy to help." I smiled.

Then Brandon got SUPERserious. "But most of all thank you for helping me with Holly and her pups. You've been just . . . AWESOME!" he gushed as he brushed his shaggy bangs out of his eyes.

Then he, like . . . stared right into the . . . murky depths of my . . . fragile but tortured . . . soul.

OMG! I thought I was going to MELT into a big puddle of sticky goo right there at the front desk.

# SQUEEEEEEE ☺!!

I decided to be perfectly honest with Brandon because TRUE friendship is based on honesty, trust, and mutual respect. Right?!

"Thanks, Brandon! I have to admit I've had some challenging moments with the dogs. But overall things have gone really well, and they've been a lot of fun!"

Okay, so maybe I wasn't COMPLETELY honest.

Yes, I know! I very conveniently left out the fact that my mom had told me I COULDN'T dog sit but

I had done it anyway and kept the dogs hidden in my bedroom.

And I didn't mention how my mom had decided to stay home this morning, which meant I couldn't leave the dogs at the house as originally planned.

I also skipped the part about me bringing the dogs to school today.

And the fact that Chloe, Zoey, and I had hidden them in the janitor's closet.

And how Marcy had helped us smuggle them into Principal Winston's office while he was out for the day.

So I guess you could say I basically LIED to Brandon by NOT telling him things. Sort of.

But get THIS! He said he planned to thank me for all of my help by getting us cupcakes at the CupCakery sometime soon!

# SQUEEEEEEEE ☺!!

I was really happy to hear that news (and so were those nosy snoops Chloe and Zoey!) . . .

Anyway, in less than ONE hour, we'll be meeting Marcy to pick up the dogs from the principal's office.

And then Chloe will take over.

Chloe and Zoey are both really LUCKY because THEIR parents know about the dogs. So they won't have to sneak around or hide them in their bedrooms like I did.

I'm just happy I survived the past twenty-four hours! And so did ALL the dogs!

# SQUEEEEEEEEE ☺!!

I don't mean to brag or anything.

But I've been the . . .

# PERFECT.

# PET SITTER!!

☺!!

# Okay!! MUST. NOT. PANIC ☹!!

I just got some text messages from MARCY!!

MARCY: Waiting for you guys in Winston's office. Dogs are fine. See you soon.

ME: Great! At my locker waiting for Chloe and Zoey. Should be there in about 2 minutes.

MARCY: BTW, dog water bowl is empty. Is it okay to give them more water?

ME: Please do not open dog cage. So, no water.

MARCY: Are you sure? They look thirsty.

ME: DO NOT OPEN DOG CAGE!!!!!!!!!!!!!!!!!

MARCY: OOPS!! ☹!!

ME: What happened?!!

ME: Marcy?!!!!!!!!!!!!!!!!!!!!!!!!

MARCY: HEEEEEEEELP!!!

This is what happened. . . .

MARCY OPENS THE DOG CAGE ☹!!

I was about to rush off to rescue Marcy when I heard someone calling my name.

"NIKKI! Wait up! I need to talk to you!"

Brandon jogged up and leaned on my locker, completely out of breath.

"Whew! I just ran all the way from the gym to the library, and then here. But I'm glad I caught you before you left! I forgot to mention this earlier, but is anyone at your house right now?"

That's when I got another text from Marcy.

> MARCY: Trying to put dogs back in cage. Impossible! Where are you guys?!

"Actually, Brandon, my mom is home right now. She didn't go to work today. Why do you ask?"

"Great! Since I have to be at the science fair until 7:00 this evening, I just sent the Queasy Cheesy driver to your house to pick up the dogs and take them to Chloe's house. Is that okay?"

I just stared at Brandon with my mouth dangling open. "Wait a minute! You already sent the driver to MY HOUSE?!"

"Yes," Brandon answered.

"TO PICK UP THE DOGS?!"

"Yes."

"FROM MY MOM?!!!" I practically screeched.

"Is there a problem? I thought you said she was home," Brandon asked, a little confused.

"She is home! Er, I mean, she WAS! Actually."

That's when I got another text from Marcy.

> MARCY: WHERE ARE YOU?!!!! The dogs
> are running around and getting into
> everything!! HELP!!!

"Um . . . my mom just texted me. She took the dogs . . . er, SHOPPING! They won't be back for at least an hour."

"Shopping? Really!" Brandon said. "Well, I'll just tell the driver to wait in the driveway until she gets back."

"NO! He can't! I mean, okay. But after shopping she plans to go to, um . . . the SPA!"

"Nikki, your mom is taking eight dogs shopping and to the spa?!"

"It's a DOGGIE spa! And it's run by Miss Bri-Bri. She's the lady you spoke to on the phone yesterday. They'll probably be there for, like, seventeen hours, so the driver definitely shouldn't wait!"

Then, Chloe and Zoey walked up.

"Hi, Nikki. Is everything okay?" Zoey asked.

"Yeah, you look a little flustered!" Chloe added.

"Well, things ARE a little crazy right now!" Brandon explained. "Nikki just gave me an update on the dogs. And some of it is almost unbelievable!"

"YOU TOLD BRANDON ABOUT THE DOGS?!!" Chloe and Zoey exclaimed.

"YES! I mean, NO! Sorry, I'm just really, really confused right now!" I muttered.

"Nikki told me the dogs aren't at her house right now," Brandon said.

"So you know all about us bringing the dogs to school today?!" Chloe laughed.

"And them completely trashing the janitor's closet?!" Zoey giggled.

"Nikki, why are you making those strange, ugly faces at us and pointing at Brandon?" Chloe asked.

"OOPS!" Chloe and Zoey mumbled.

That's when Brandon started to freak out. "Okay, wait a minute! Did you guys just say you brought the dogs to SCHOOL today?! And put them in the JANITOR'S CLOSET?!"

"No, we DIDN'T just say that," Chloe fibbed.

"Well, Nikki just told me her MOM was taking them SHOPPING and to a doggie SPA?!" Brandon said.

"YOUR MOM IS TAKING THE DOGS SHOPPING AND TO A DOGGIE SPA?!" Chloe and Zoey exclaimed.

"Well, yes! Of course she didn't!" I shrugged.

"Okay, Nikki! I'm really confused!" Brandon said, shaking his head. "If the dogs are NOT at your house OR in the janitor's closet OR shopping with your mom OR at the doggie spa, then WHERE in the heck ARE they?!"

Brandon, Chloe, and Zoey stared at me, like, FOREVER, waiting for my answer.

Suddenly Marcy came running down the hall, screaming at the top of her lungs! . . .

Which meant I DIDN'T have to answer Brandon's question, because MARCY did ☺!

"WHAT! The dogs are in Principal Winston's office?!! Are you guys SERIOUS?!" Brandon groaned.

"As serious as a HEART ATTACK!" we answered.

That's when the five of us frantically took off running to get to the principal's office!

☹!!

# AAAAAAAAAAAAAHHHHH!!!...

(That was me screaming.)

OMG! I was so ANGRY at myself!

WHY did I think I could secretly keep eight dogs in my bedroom? And then take them to school? And hide them in the janitor's closet? And then smuggle them into the principal's office?

WHAT was I thinking?!!!!

And just when I thought things couldn't get any worse, they did.

When the five of us finally arrived at the principal's office, we cautiously peeked inside. Unfortunately, we saw eight dogs running loose, trashing the office.

AND one very confused, ticked-off principal . . .

Of course, when Principal Winston saw us standing there, he totally lost it! "Can anyone explain to me WHY there's a pack of WILD DOGS running loose in my office?!" he yelled.

"I'm sorry, sir! But it's ALL my f-fault!" I stammered.

"No, it's actually MY fault!" Marcy said, hanging her head.

"Principal Winston, I accept total responsibility for these dogs," Brandon admitted solemnly.

"Well, I was involved too, sir!" Zoey said glumly.

That's when everyone stared at Chloe.

"Hey, I just raided your candy jar!" Chloe shrugged. "I'm no puppy smuggler!"

I could NOT believe Chloe was throwing ALL of us under the bus like that!!

"Well, the owner of these dogs better speak up, or I'm going to be calling ALL of your parents!!"

It got SO quiet you could hear a pin drop. Then we heard a friendly voice in the doorway. . . .

EXCUSE ME, PRINCIPAL WINSTON, BUT THESE DOGS ARE PART OF MY SCIENCE FAIR PROJECT, AND SOMEHOW THEY ESCAPED! I'M REALLY SORRY ABOUT THAT!

IT WAS MAX CRUMBLY?!!

Of course, everyone was shocked to see him standing there. And poor Principal Winston was so confused, he didn't know WHO to believe. Until Max called Holly over and all eight dogs tackled him and smothered him with kisses. . . .

Max introduced himself to the principal and told him he attended South Ridge Middle School.

He went on to explain that his science fair project with Brandon was Using Distillation to Turn Dirty Water into Clean Drinking Water.

And it involved taking dirty runoff water from compost, and bathwater (from the dogs), and turning it into clean drinking water.

Principal Winston was VERY impressed with both Max AND his science project. And apparently, so were Chloe, Zoey, and Marcy. For some unknown reason, all THREE of them suddenly got a severe case of the giggles.

I could NOT believe that they were actually FLIRTING with Max like that.

Anyway, while Principal Winston chatted with Max, Brandon started to gather up the dogs and put them back in their cage, and Chloe, Zoey, and Marcy tidied up the office.

MAX, DISTRACTING PRINCIPAL WINSTON
WHILE WE DID DAMAGE CONTROL!

As Max was about to leave, he and Brandon exchanged glances.

Then Brandon cleared his throat.

"Actually, Principal Winston, if it's okay with you, maybe we can help Max with the dogs."

"Yeah, we definitely wouldn't want them to get loose during the science fair!" I added.

"That's a good idea!" Principal Winston agreed. "So why don't all of you help Max keep an eye on them!"

"Now that I think about it, I'll probably just take the dogs home before they cause any more trouble," Max reasoned.

"Actually, Max, I like THAT idea even better!" Principal Winston chuckled.

Brandon grabbed the wagon, and the six of us got the heck out of there!

Once we had made it out into the hall with the dogs, everyone was SO relieved! We actually high-fived each other.

"Nice work, Crumbly!" Brandon exclaimed.

"OMG! I thought Principal Winston was going to call our parents for sure!" I sputtered. "I almost peed my pants!"

Of course everyone laughed at my silly joke.

"Which reminds me," Brandon said, "I still need to call the driver and tell him NOT to pick up the dogs from your house, Nikki!" He took out his cell phone. "I'll just have him come to the school instead!"

Anyway, I managed to survive yet another CATASTROPHE! Thanks to MAX CRUMBLY!

That guy is actually pretty COOL!

☺!!!
...

## FRIDAY—4:45 P.M.
## AT CHLOE'S HOUSE

Right now I'm so completely EXHAUSTED from all of the drama with the dogs that I could fall over!

After we left the principal's office, Chloe rushed home to get ready for the dogs.

And since Brandon had to be at the science fair, I agreed to help deliver them to Chloe's house.

I have to admit, I was SUPERrelieved that I DIDN'T have to HIDE them from my parents anymore.

It was a miracle I was actually able to keep the dogs hidden in my bedroom without them finding out.

After a very noisy trip with the dogs in a van, I anxiously rang Chloe's doorbell.

*DING-DONG! DING-DONG! DING-DONG!*

The first thing I planned to do when I got back home was relax in a warm bubble bath ☺!

No, wait! The upstairs bathroom still reeked of manure and peanut butter ☹. EWW!!

Okay. Instead, I'd just chillax by finishing up a watercolor painting I'd started last weekend.

But that was going to be difficult to do since the dogs had chewed a leg off my artist easel ☹.

Well, I could always lounge around in my comfy pj's and bunny slippers and just write in my diary ☺.

NOT! The dogs had accidentally peed on my pj's and chewed the ears off my bunny slippers ☹. So now they looked like big fuzzy rats (my bunny slippers, not the dogs)!

My thoughts were interrupted when someone finally answered the door. The person was wearing a surgical mask, surgical scrubs, and latex gloves, and was holding a can of spray cleaner. . . .

ME, WONDERING WHY CHLOE WAS
DRESSED SO STRANGELY?!

"Hi, Nikki. Yeah, it's me. Did you get my phone message? I'm really sorry," she said glumly.

I burst into giggles.

"Hey there, Doc McStuffins! Did I catch you in the middle of surgery?" I teased.

Chloe pulled down her face mask and glared at me.

"No, Miss Smarty-Pants! I sneezed and it freaked out my uncle. So now he's forcing me to wear this getup AND spray the room with disinfectant," she complained. "He's a total germophobe! He just got here a few hours ago and is refusing to go back to his condo because his next-door neighbor just adopted a . . . um, D-O-G!"

"WHAT?! Chloe, why did you spell 'dog'?"

"Shhhhh!" she hissed, and looked over her shoulder nervously. "That word will practically send my uncle into convulsions. So we have to be VERY careful what we say."

"Chloe! Who's at the door?!" I heard a man yell from the kitchen. "Please tell them they can't come inside without a face mask and latex gloves. We have enough germs in this house!"

"Just stop worrying, Uncle Carlos! Please!" Chloe answered, a little irritated.

He continued. . . .

"And if it's the mailman, please call the Centers for Disease Control! Heaven knows what deadly germs are living on those spit-covered envelopes people have licked that he carries from house to house. He's probably spreading the bubonic plague! I'm getting heart palpitations just thinking about it!"

"Uncle Carlos, it's just my friend Nikki," she replied. "PLEASE! Just chill out!"

"How can I NOT worry when you're standing there with the door open? Do you realize you're letting in dozens of airborne viruses every minute? No wonder I'm feeling really sick!" he complained as he sprayed the room. . . .

CHLOE'S UNCLE CARLOS IS
A LITTLE, UM . . . WEIRD!

"Sorry, Nikki. Just ignore him!" she whispered. "So, what's up?"

"Chloe, I HEARD that!" he yelled. "In spite of my nasal congestion and severe ear infection from my allergies, I can STILL hear!"

Chloe rolled her eyes in frustration.

"Um, actually, Chloe," I began, "I just came by to drop off these, um . . . eight packages . . . just like we discussed," I said awkwardly, and pointed to the dogs.

"So I guess you DIDN'T get the message I left on your cell phone," Chloe sighed.

"What message?" I asked. "I guess I didn't hear my phone ring. The dogs were SUPERnoisy on the trip over here."

Chloe cringed when I said the word "dogs."

"OOPS!" I muttered. "Sorry!"

"DOGS?!" her uncle gasped. "Did someone just say 'DOGS'?! Take them away before I break out in a rash! Oh no! I'm already starting to itch!"

"No, Uncle Carlos! Nikki said 'DAWGS'! It's just a slang word for 'friends,'" Chloe fibbed. "Hey, Nikki, can you help me out here?" she whispered, nudging my arm.

"Yo! Listen up, Chloe!" I suddenly exclaimed very loudly. "Me and my dawgs will be chillin' at Crazy Burger tonight. You down with that?"

Startled, the smallest puppy looked up at me and barked. Chloe and I both shushed her.

"Chloe! Did I just hear a DOG?!" her uncle yelled.

He coughed overdramatically. "Now I'm getting light-headed and short of breath! It's probably an asthma attack! Chloe, quick, call 911!"

"Uncle Carlos, you DON'T have asthma!" Chloe grumbled. "Besides, you've already made me call 911 three times in the past hour. They've probably blocked our phone number by now!"

"Then use your cell phone!" her uncle argued. "And just because I don't have asthma right now doesn't mean I won't get it later today!"

Chloe looked like she was about to lose it!

"How about I babysit the dogs and YOU babysit my uncle?" she mumbled under her breath.

"I HEARD that!" her uncle shouted again. "Are you SURE there are no DOGS in this house?!"

"Seriously, Nikki, I'm SO sorry!" Chloe apologized. "My parents said I couldn't keep the dogs anymore because my uncle is going to be here for the weekend. And, unfortunately, he says he's allergic to dogs. And just about EVERYTHING else!"

"Don't worry, Chloe. I totally understand," I assured her.

"How about Zoey? Maybe she can keep the dogs for two days?" Chloe suggested.

"I don't think so. Today is her mom's birthday, and Zoey is taking her out to dinner. They'll be gone most of the evening. So I guess I'll just keep them at my house another day." I sighed.

My stomach was already twisting into knots at the thought of hiding the dogs from my parents again.

Although I was exhausted, I felt even more sorry for Chloe.

I'd much rather spend the weekend with a pack of wild dogs than her whiny, slightly nutty, germophobic uncle Carlos.

Chloe offered to help load the dogs.

As we walked out to the van, Chloe's mom was coming in.

"Hi, Mrs. Garcia." I smiled.

"Hi, Mom," Chloe said. "And don't worry! Holly and her puppies were just leaving."

"Hi, girls! WOW! The PUPPIES are ADORABLE!" Mrs. Garcia squealed. "Well, I've got some great news for you both!"

ME, HOPING THE GREAT NEWS IS THAT
UNCLE CARLOS IS GOING HOME!!

"The Daisy Girl Scouts are having a sleepover at a neighbor's house to earn their pet care badges. So, Nikki, if it's okay with you, their troop leader, who is also my sister, would LOVE to babysit the dogs since Chloe can't do it."

"I think that's a great idea!" Chloe exclaimed. "And tomorrow, after the sleepover, Mom and I can pick up the dogs and take them to Zoey's house. I know you're exhausted and need a break, Nikki!"

Mrs. Garcia continued. "My sister loves dogs and has one of her own. So Holly and her puppies will be in good hands. And it'll be a great experience for the sixteen little girls. Who knows! You might even find a home for one of the pups."

"Actually, that sounds fantastic to me, too!" I said excitedly. "I'll just run this past Brandon to make sure it's okay with him!"

I called Brandon on my cell phone and explained the situation with Chloe's uncle and how Mrs. Garcia's sister had volunteered to watch the dogs (along with her Daisy troop). Brandon was totally sold on the idea.

So everything is all set!

Mrs. Garcia agreed to drop the dogs off at the sleepover and then drive me home.

It looks like my doggie DRAMA is over and I SURVIVED!

# SQUEEEEEEEEEEEE!!!

☺!!

# I CAN'T BELIEVE I'M ACTUALLY HERE!
## AGAIN ☹!!

Brianna and I had fallen in love with ALL the dogs, but our favorite was the smallest puppy.

She was SUPERcute, curious, and smart, and loved to play with Brianna's stuffed animals.

Although I was really going to miss taking care of the dogs, I felt proud I had been able to help keep them safe.

I also learned that puppies can be as rambunctious as they are CUTE.

Calling Holly's seven puppies a handful was an understatement.

They were like seven tiny Tasmanian devils with puppy breath and no potty-training skills whatsoever.

I was already looking forward to seeing them at Fuzzy Friends next week.

Anyway, Chloe and I had no idea where the sleepover was going to be. But as soon as Mrs. Garcia pulled into the driveway, Chloe and I instantly recognized the house.

At first we totally FREAKED.

Then we stared in shock.

Soon we started to snicker.

And then we giggled.

Finally we laughed until our sides hurt!

Between the eight dogs and the sixteen Daisy Girl Scouts (including MY bratty little sister, Brianna), we felt really, really sorry for . . .

# MACKENZIE HOLLISTER!! . . .

Sorry, but MacKenzie totally deserved every fun-filled ~~puppy~~ poopy moment!

It was going to be one VERY, VERY long night.

Especially after I suggested to Brianna that Miss Bri-Bri open a new PAW SPA right inside MacKenzie's very huge and luxurious bedroom!

Then she could provide her peanut butter facials to MacKenzie's little sister, Amanda, the fourteen other girls, AND the seven dogs for FREE!

Just kidding ☺!!

# NOT!!

I am such an evil GENIUS!

# MWA-HA-HA-HA-HA!

# ☺!!

## SATURDAY, MAY 3—5:00 P.M.
## AT BRIANNA'S BALLET CLASS

I was so exhausted from taking care of the dogs that I slept past breakfast and lunch.

And by the time I came downstairs to grab a bite to eat, Brianna had gotten home from her sleepover and left the house again to go to ballet practice.

Which meant I hadn't gotten a chance to talk to her all day.

I was absolutely DYING to know how everything went with the puppies. And her new PAW SPA ☺!

Mom told me Brianna really enjoyed the sleepover and taking care of the puppies. And she had earned a pet care badge, which meant she'd be a responsible pet owner.

Anyway, I decided to ride with Mom to pick up Brianna from ballet practice.

And when I went inside to get my sister, I heard some very SCANDALOUS news!

But first let me make one thing perfectly clear.

I'm definitely not the type who spreads nasty RUMORS about other people.

And I refuse to GOSSIP behind a person's back (unlike most of the CCPs—the Cute, Cool & Popular kids—who will gossip about you right to your FACE).

But I couldn't RESIST getting the latest DIRT on a certain diary-stealing drama queen who had just transferred to North Hampton Hills International Academy.

And it came from a VERY reliable source.

Namely, MacKenzie's little sister, AMANDA.

I was just minding my own business and trying to be friendly when I said . . .

ME, TALKING TO MACKENZIE'S
LITTLE SISTER, AMANDA!

"Well, Amanda, if it's a secret, then you don't have to tell me," I said, giving her a reassuring hug. "But I'm VERY sure Santa is going to bring YOU and your BFF, Brianna, lots of fun toys this year because you're the sweetest LITTLE sister a BIG sister could EVER have!!" I ~~tied~~ gushed.

"You really think so?!" Amanda giggled. "Okay, so the big secret about MacKenzie is—"

"Wait a minute!" Brianna interrupted, smiling at me like a snake in a pink tutu. "Since we're both such sweet little sisters, will you take Amanda and me to see *Princess Sugar Plum Saves Baby Unicorn Island, Part 9?!* PLEEEASE?!"

"Wow! A Princess Sugar Plum Movie?! That would be AWESOME!" Amanda squealed.

I gave Brianna a dirty look.

I could NOT believe she was taking advantage of me like this.

But if I wanted to get the lowdown on MacKenzie, I didn't have a choice but to give in to Brianna's demands.

"Um, okay. But, Amanda, we have to ask your mom first," I explained. "Now, let's get back to MacKenzie's big secret, okay? So SPILL IT!"

Amanda took a deep breath and began a second time. "Well, when MacKenzie went to her new school, she—"

"Hold on!" Brianna interrupted. "We're going to need some hot, buttery popcorn at the movie."

"FINE!" I said, annoyed. "I'll get you popcorn!"

"And gummy bears, too!" Brianna added.

That little brat was milking this situation like a dairy cow.

I could NOT believe I was being so blatantly manipulated by my own GREEDY little sister!

Like, WHO does that?!!

"OKAY! And gummy bears, too!" I said through gritted teeth. "But nothing more. That's it! Do you understand?"

Brianna grinned at me like a baby shark. . . .

Nikki, you're the BEST sister EVER!!

"Now, Amanda, where were we before Brianna so RUDELY interrupted us?"

Amanda lowered her voice to a whisper.

Then she told me some of the things that had happened to MacKenzie at her new school.

# OMG!

# The stuff she said was UNBELIEVABLE!

No wonder MacKenzie had been acting so weird when we saw her at the CupCakery.

I ALMOST felt SORRY for her!

Notice I said "almost."

Anyway, I have to stop writing in my diary now.

To celebrate Brianna earning her pet care badge, Mom is letting us have dinner at Crazy Burger!!

# SQUEEEEEEEEE ☺!

I'm so hungry right now, I could eat one of those silly Styrofoam Crazy Burger hats, googly eyes and all!

☺!!

I just talked to Zoey on the phone an hour ago.
She told me that Chloe had dropped the dogs off
around noon, and Zoey has been having a blast
with them all day.

It seems so QUIET in MY bedroom now that the
dogs are gone. I really miss them.

Anyway, I'm still in shock about the stuff I heard
about MacKenzie today.

Apparently, her first day of school went fine and
everyone was SUPERfriendly. But her second day
was a disaster.

MacKenzie was in the bathroom when a group of the
most popular girls in the entire school came in. They
were laughing really hard about something, and she
heard them mention her name.

So MacKenzie peeked out of her stall and . . .

. . . CAUGHT THEM LAUGHING AND MAKING
FUN OF THAT VIDEO OF HER WITH
THE BUG IN HER HAIR!!

MACKENZIE WAS SO EMBARRASSED
AND HUMILIATED THAT SHE HID OUT
IN THAT BATHROOM STALL FOR THREE HOURS,
UNTIL SCHOOL WAS OVER!!

And then she ended up with a one-hour after-school detention for skipping class!!

Amanda said MacKenzie HATED the popular kids at North Hampton Hills because they were mean, snobby, and made fun of her because of the bug video.

OMG! All of that mean-girl drama sounded uncomfortably familiar. MacKenzie was being treated by those North Hampton Hills girls EXACTLY the same way SHE treated ME!

Apparently, some of the kids at her new school had labeled MacKenzie Hollister, THE former Queen Bee of the CCPs . . .

# A BIG DORK!

Well, MacKenzie, welcome to the club ☺!

All of this is just SO unbelievably, um . . .

# UNBELIEVABLE!!

Because this sounded NOTHING like the CCP MEAN GIRL who'd had a locker next to mine for eight very long months at WCD.

Come on! WHO in their right mind WOULDN'T love attending a swanky school like North Hampton Hills International Academy?!

But Amanda said MacKenzie made up cool stuff about her life and pretended to be someone else so the students there would like her. Which also explains why she had all but stolen MY identity when I met some of her friends at the CupCakery.

Anyway, my conversation with Amanda was very RUDELY interrupted by a loud, shrill voice.

"AMANDA!! I told you to NEVER talk to that little BRAT or her PATHETIC sister again! Let's go! NOW!!" MacKenzie shrieked.

Then she swooped in like a vicious . . . um, vulture, and dragged Amanda away like a . . . dead carcass. . . .

MACKENZIE GRABS AMANDA
AND DRAGS HER AWAY!

That's when a smile slowly spread across Brianna's face.

"It looks like MacKenzie is still mad about the Paw Spa I set up in her bedroom during our sleepover!" Brianna giggled. "Everybody LOVED it! Except MacKenzie."

And get this! MacKenzie didn't say a single word to me!!

She just sashayed away with her nose stuck in the air like I didn't even exist.

I just HATE it when that girl sashays!!

Anyway, it's partially Brianna's fault that I didn't get even more details about what happened. Amanda couldn't complete a full sentence without Brianna rudely interrupting to demand assorted unhealthy movie snacks.

So if I want to get more DIRT on MacKenzie, it looks like I might actually have to spend an

afternoon taking Brianna and Amanda to Princess
Sugar Plum Saves Baby Unicorn Island, Part 9.

Suffering through yet another of those silly,
mind-numbing Princess Sugar Plum movies would be
worth it just to stay one step ahead of MacKenzie
and her DRAMAFEST.

☺!!

Brandon called me earlier today with some really great news about Fuzzy Friends!

According to the manager, four dogs had been picked up for adoption on Friday and six on Saturday.

So as of this morning, Fuzzy Friends had ten openings for new animals!!

# SQUEEEEEEEE ☺!!!

Which meant that there was FINALLY enough space for Holly and her seven puppies!

But this is the crazy part!

# ALL THE PUPPIES HAVE ALREADY BEEN ADOPTED!!! AND HOLLY, TOO!!

The vet said Holly had pretty much weaned her puppies and they were eating solid puppy food.

I felt really happy and sad at the same time! I would have LOVED to have gotten a dog of my own.

But after my mom made such a big fuss about her new furniture and carpet, I didn't even bother to ask.

Mrs. Garcia's sister adopted Holly, and FOUR puppies were adopted by the girls at the pet care sleepover! WOW!!

So thanks to Chloe's uncle Carlos, five dogs found homes!

And Marcy got a puppy, and two puppies went to people on the Fuzzy Friends waiting list for golden retrievers.

I felt a little heartbroken knowing those wonderful dogs had been placed with OTHER families.

I guess MY family would NEVER, EVER get a dog!

I couldn't help but blink back tears.

I know it's crazy to have grown so attached to them after just a few days.

But I feel depressed looking at the outline in the carpet where their cage used to be.

My room is so quiet now, I can barely sleep at all!

Brianna has been missing the puppies too.

Even though I made her swear on her Princess Sugar Plum Pink Baby Unicorn to keep the puppies a BIG SECRET, lately it's been the ONLY thing she talks about.

"You know who'd really LOVE these meatballs?" she sighed sadly at the dinner table earlier today. "Holly and her seven little puppies that we hid in Nikki's room! I really miss them."

One part of me wanted to reach across the table
and slap her. And the other part of me was so
freaked out that I choked on a meatball.

Well, actually . . . ALL of me was choking on that meatball!

"Nikki!" Mom cried. "Are you okay?!"

I coughed and quickly guzzled my glass of punch to wash the meatball down before my face turned blue.

"Sorry about that! These meatballs are so delicious, I'm literally trying to inhale them!" I giggled nervously.

Mom and Dad traded glances with each other.

"Now, what were you saying about puppies?" Dad asked Brianna curiously.

"Hey, Brianna!" I interrupted, trying desperately to change the subject. "How is Oliver doing? I bet he really likes meatballs too!"

"He LOVES puppies MORE!" she said glumly. "He said he wanted to play with the puppies you had in your room."

Dad furrowed his brow. "So, are these Princess Sugar Plum stuffed puppies?"

"No, Dad! They're Nikki's puppies! And they are REAL!" Brianna corrected him.

"Actually, Dad, the puppies aren't real," I explained. "But Brianna likes to pretend they live in my bedroom."

"Nuh-uh!!" she protested. "They're real and you know it! Remember the torn-up pillows in the family room? And the peanut butter and mud from the Paw Spa in the upstairs bathroom? And the dog poop in Mommy and Daddy's room? And the—"

"HA! HA! HA!" I roared over the sound of her snitching on me. "Dogs pooping in Mom and Dad's room?! OMG! You're HILARIOUS, Brianna!"

"You weren't laughing when you were lying on the middle of the bathroom floor, covered with mud, peanut butter, and toilet water!" she yelled, and stuck her tongue out at me.

"Brianna!" Mom scolded her. "That's enough!"

I could NOT believe that little BRAT was putting all of my personal business in the streets like that!

Thanks a million, Brianna!

Just throw me under the bus so Mom and Dad will ground me until my eighteenth birthday.

"I don't have the slightest idea WHY Brianna has suddenly been so obsessed with puppies lately," I shrugged, all innocentlike. "Maybe it was that pet care sleepover."

Dad and Mom exchanged glances again.

Actually, I was starting to feel a little uneasy.

I couldn't help but notice that my parents were acting kind of weird too.

Did they actually believe Brianna's crazy story?

"Nikki, after dinner I'd like you to help me bring in some groceries from the car, okay?" Mom said.

Twenty minutes later, I was carrying in a half dozen bags from Pets-N-Stuff.

"These are groceries?" I asked skeptically. "Mom, I know you've caught Brianna drinking out of the toilet and biting the mailman once or twice! But feeding her Doggy Diner puppy chow is a bit drastic, don't you think?!"

"It's a pet food drive for Brianna's troop," Mom said.

"Hey! What's this stuff?" Brianna asked. "Mom, did you buy me some puppy chow cereal? YUM!"

I couldn't believe Brianna actually said that.

"I ate lots of bacon doggie snacks when Nikki babysat me and the puppies," she bragged.

Then Dad came downstairs, carrying a big white box with a huge red bow on it.

"WOW!" I gasped. Was it a new laptop computer to replace the one Brianna had put in the dishwasher?

GIRLS! WE HAVE A BIG SURPRISE FOR YOU!

We opened the box and peeked inside!! . . .

The wiggly little puppy jumped into our arms and licked our faces.

It was Holly's smallest pup! The one that Brianna and I had fallen in love with!

"SQUEEEEEEEEEEEEEEEEEE!!" we both squealed.

"YIP! YIP! YIP! YIP!" the puppy barked.

We were SO happy, we both started to CRY!

"I've been begging your mom for a dog for a long time now, and she finally gave in!" Dad boasted. "You girls can thank me later!"

"Well, both of you have been talking about dogs nonstop all week. It made me seriously consider getting one. And when I picked up Brianna from her sleepover and saw THIS little puppy! I couldn't help but fall in love with her. I called Fuzzy Friends right away and arranged to adopt her!"

"Can we call her DAISY?!" Brianna asked excitedly. "She's the littlest, cutest, most sweetest dog in the entire world!"

I totally agreed. We were so happy and excited that we did a group hug! With DAISY! . . .

THE MAXWELL FAMILY'S NEW PUPPY!!

"Something told me she was the right dog!" Mom said, winking at Dad.

A wave of paranoia swept over me. Now, what did THAT little comment mean?!

I thought I had just gotten away with the biggest doggie-smuggling operation in Maxwell family history!

But now I was starting to wonder if it was Mom and Dad who'd pulled a fast one on Brianna and me.

Anyway, Holly and her pups had new homes!

WE had an adorable new puppy named Daisy!

And my next week at school was going to be DRAMA FREE for the first time all year!!

My life was PERFECT ☺!!

Until I got a copy of a parent e-mail from Principal Winston. . . .

TO: Mr. and Mrs. Maxwell

FROM: Principal Winston

RE: Eighth-Grade Student Exchange Week

Dear Parents,

Each year, all eighth-grade students at WCD Middle School participate in a Student Exchange Week with local schools. We feel this helps to foster community and good citizenship with both students and faculty at the host schools.

Your child, Nikki Maxwell, will be attending NORTH HAMPTON HILLS INTERNATIONAL ACADEMY along with several other WCD students. Everyone is expected to be on their best behavior, to follow the student handbook of the host school, and to make WDC proud. More information about this very important event will be sent home with students next week. If you have any questions or concerns, please feel free to contact me.

Sincerely,

Principal Winston

At first I thought the letter was some kind of PRANK. But when I checked the WCD calendar on our school website, sure enough, the Student Exchange Week was listed as an official event.

# JUST GREAT ☹!!

So now I'm going to be attending school with MacKenzie Hollister?!!

Just when I thought that drama queen was out of my life FOREVER, she shows up AGAIN like a recurring NIGHTMARE!

Although, from what I've heard, I think she could probably use my help! Hey, it's really TOUGH when other kids make you feel like an outsider.

But you just have to believe in YOURSELF!! How do I know this? Probably because . . .

# I'M SUCH A DORK!
# ☺!!

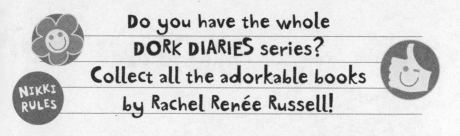

# Do you have the whole DORK DIARIES series?
## Collect all the adorkable books by Rachel Renée Russell!

NIKKI RULES

Dork Diaries | Dork Diaries: Party Time | Dork Diaries: Pop Star | Dork Diaries: Skating Sensation | Dork Diaries: Dear Dork | Dork Diaries: Holiday Hearbreak

Dork Diaries: TV Star | Dork Diaries: Once Upon a Dork | Dork Diaries: Drama Queen | Dork Diaries: Puppy Love | Dork Diaries: Once Upon a Dork | Dork Diaries: Drama Queen

Dork Diaries: Frenemies Forever | Dork Diaries: Crush Catastrophe | Dork Diaries: Birthday Drama | Dork Diaries: How to Dork Your Diary | Dork Diaries: OMG! All About Me Diary

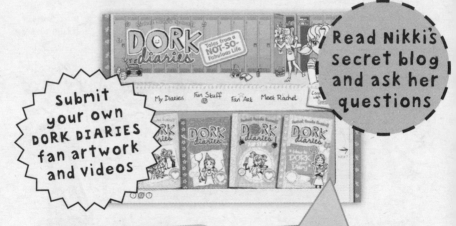

# more dorky fun!

Now you can find DORK DIARIES on Facebook and twitter too!

connect with other fans of the series!

# Rachel Renée Russell is the #1
New York Times bestselling author of the blockbuster book series Dork Diaries and the bestselling new series The Misadventures of Max Crumbly.

There are thirty million copies of her books in print worldwide, and they have been translated into thirty-seven languages.

She enjoys working with her two daughters, Erin and Nikki, who help write and illustrate her books.

Rachel's message is "Always let your inner dork shine through!"